BITTER WATER
BOOK 2 IN DR CHARLIE MANSON AOTEA...
BY LESLIE TARR

The characters in this story are not based on any specific individuals living or dead.
The locations used within this story are based on locations in New Zealand, and artistic license has been taken with the activities which take place in these locations for the purpose of dramatic enhancement of the plot.

I have never been to New Zealand, and one day when I retire, I may well go over there to check the place out. The New Zealanders have some novel and inventive approaches to criminal justice especially around the area of family involvement in justice solutions, and I hope to explore some of this in the stories within this book.

DEDICATION

I dedicate this book to a dear friend who passed away recently, at a very young age. Lovely family man who read the stories and used to 'encourage' me to get the next one out there.
I'll keep them coming for you John.

-------- 0 --------

Thanks also to my wife to my wife Katherine and pet Chihuahua Pancho the pooch, for encouragement, proofreading skills [Katherine] and bringing me treats when I come home [Pancho] which I am only shown and not allowed to take. It's the thought that counts.
I would also acknowledge Martin Dunsmuir for a sanity check of the story. I hope the people of Aotearoa will forgive my literary license in writing about their beautiful land, so much like my native Scotland. One day I would like to visit there but for the moment I have only seen from afar and through Google Earth.
As a writer the challenge is to not just come up with story lines but characters. The two retired officers are drawn from two former colleagues, and yes they did look good in Lycra. Queenie is a different story, her spirit and wisdom will be recognized by family I'm sure.
Some Maori terms used:
MANUHIRI - VISITOR
Nau mai – WELCOME
Tēnā koe – FORMAL GREETING TO A SINGLE PERSON.
Kei te pēhea koe? – How are you?
Kei te pai ahau – I am good
Me koe? – And you?
Karani - Granny

Chapter 1: Meeting at a Party

'Charlie, let me introduce Jacqueline Blackman and Miles Anderson, they are from the Maxim Environmental Managers Corporation, a company I am hoping to do some business with,' Brian introduced his guests. 'Ms Blackman is the Head of Corporate Projects and Miles is the CEO.'

'Pleased to meet a real live hero', Anderson held out his hand in greeting.

'Nice to meet you both,' Charlie shook hands with both guests. 'I would not call myself a hero,' Charlie smiled at the elegant visitor. 'Pardon my shortness it's been a busy few days and tonight is for relaxing. Anyway I am trying to forget about all that thanks, I am just here to lecture and pass on knowledge.'

'We understand entirely, Charles,' Anderson said. 'It must have been quite an ordeal. So how are you finding New Zealand otherwise?'

'Fine, I'm enjoying it very much,' Charlie bristled at the name, 'and it's Charlie.'

'Of course, the other fellow,' Miles replied. 'I forgot you prefer not to be associated with . . . well, you know.'

'Yes I know,' Charlie replied.

'Perhaps we can start again,' Ms Blackman said. 'Charlie how much do you know about environmental criminology?'

'Well, let me see,' Charlie retorted, 'crime tends to have four elements, a law, an offender, a victim or target and of course a place. Environmental criminology is concerned with the latter being place and crimes. Do I pass the test?'

'Yes, top of the class Dr Manson,' Ms Blackman showed her displeasure. 'We were rather hoping you could come along and give a talk to our corporate division on criminology and the environmental aspects, if you are interested. It pays a fee, and we rather hoped you might be able to advise us on a situation we're dealing with at the moment.

We are interested in hiring your services as a consultant, perhaps you could give us a call in a day or so once you are rested and we can discuss some business,' Ms Blackman handed Charlie her card. 'Yes I am sure we can meet up,' Charlie took a sip of his drink.

'Bitter water... sorry this drink's just a bit bitter; I will give you a call to arrange to meet. You must excuse me I am just a bit nonplussed at the moment, exploding muskets you understand.'

With that Charlie shook both their hands again and wandered off to seek out Barry Goodman.

'Interesting fellow your brother-in-law, Brian,' Anderson said. 'I am sure he is just what we are looking for.'

-------- 0 --------

'So what was that all about?' Debbie asked.

'Not sure, sis' Charlie replied, 'but Queenie warned me about those two as they walked over, and I trust her. They are after something.' 'I'll have a word with Brian,' Debbie replied. 'Do we ask the Warkworth irregulars to stick around?'

'If they do you will know there is trouble and Queenie has our backs,' Charlie joked.

'Anyway it's time for folks to dine,' Debbie said moving off to round up the guests to start eating the vast buffet she had prepared with her daughters.

'Nice looking lady there, Doctor Charlie,' Pinkie Lumo said as he stood eating his plate of buffet food. 'Do you know her?'
'No Pinkie, she is from the Maxim Corporation,' Charlie replied. 'Ever come across them?'

'Not a group I have heard of,' Pinkie looked at Charlie quizzically. 'Is it something for the police to be interested in, you look intrigued?'
'Not sure yet,' Charlie looked at the DS, 'but your Grandma has warned me to be careful about Bitter Water. Does that mean anything to you?'

'No,' Pinkie replied, 'but you know Queenie. It could be something or nothing, more likely something.'

'I know,' Charlie said, 'and that worries me.'

Chapter 2: Rest day

Charlie woke late for him at 9 a.m. Sunday morning. He was spending the day at his sister's after the dinner party the night before. His plans were straightforward, rest, eat, read and rest, before heading back to Auckland and the next week of lectures at the Summer School.

Today he hoped his plans would be fulfilled.

'Uncle Charlie, sorry, just Charlie,' Chrissie approached her uncle who was sitting in the garden reading his kindle. 'We wondered if you fancied a little drive.'

'We as in whom?' Charlie asked.

'Gisele and me,' Chrissie replied. 'There is a nice spot down by Bream Bay. We thought we could take a little picnic, nothing to spoil our appetites for later, a couple of deck chairs and sit by the sea and read.'

Debbie watched her daughter with great interest. She knew something was going on that she could not work out.
'Okay, let me get this straight,' Charlie said. 'You want to spend some time sitting by the bay reading with your old uncle.'

'Yes.'

'Are there some boys you want to meet and I am a chaperone?'

'No.'

'You are grounded unless you have an irresponsible adult with you and you chose me?'
'No, and yes you are an irresponsible adult.'
'Okay the uncle in me is saying *ah aren't they nice*, but the profiler in me tells me I am being had, what's the catch?'

'Well it is about an hour each way and Gisele and I could do with the driving practice.'

'Okay now we have it, you want me to sit in a car with two learner drivers and risk my life.'

'Well you have just faced a psychopath and a loaded ancient musket that blew up and killed him, so what are you worried about?'

'Okay get ready I will go and change into something more suitable. 'Sucker,' Debbie said laughing, 'just be back for Sunday lunch.'

-------- 0 --------

Charlie was actually delighted to spend time with his nieces and hear all about their plans and activities. The drive to Bream Bay was spectacular at this time of year, the greenery and hills were lush. The spot the girls had in mind was just beside Ruakaka. The spot was as lovely as they'd said and the trio enjoyed sitting in the sun chatting and laughing.

'You know I could get used to living here I think,' Charlie said. 'Do you mean you would leave Cullen and move here Charlie?' Gisele asked. 'Well this could be a momentous day indeed.'

'Well now I come to think of it, no,' Charlie said with a smile, 'but this place makes you think.

So what's to the north of here?'

'Well there is the oil refinery and Northport cargo depot, not as attractive,' Chrissie replied, 'and of course there is one of the Maxim depots run by the lovely Ms Blackman.'

'Oh yes,' Charlie said.

'So you did notice she was a looker, Charlie?' Gisele quizzed her uncle.

'I did indeed, but she is not my type,' Charlie said.

'So just what is your type?' Gisele asked. 'We can keep our eyes peeled for you.'

'Nice try, you pair of minxes,' Charlie laughed. 'At the moment I have no type and am not looking to discover one, but if you do see Lucy Liu around the district let me know.'

'Ah the mysterious oriental type,' Chrissie said, 'we will keep an eye out.'

Their picnic was disturbed by a noise from the bay, and they walked down to the water to see what the commotion was all about. A group of locals had gathered and were pulling dead fish out of the water.

'It's that Maxim plant you know, they are poisoning the water making it bitter,' one of the local men announced.

Charlie walked over to the group of men and asked what they were meaning.

'Well the tide brings these fish in from the bay where that Maxim company is drilling for shale gas,' the leader of the group said. 'This has been happening for weeks now, and people are eating the fish and getting sick.'
'Has anyone reported this to the authorities?' Charlie asked.
'No they are in bed with the company,' an elderly man replied. 'As always, it is the Maori who suffer for the incomer's poisonous way.'

'Uncle Charlie we will be late back,' Gisele said, 'and anyway I can see a look in your eye Mum will not like.'

-------- 0 --------

Back at the Wakefields over Sunday lunch Charlie was strangely quiet. This had not gone unnoticed by his sister and brother-in-law.

'Penny for them Charlie,' Brian asked, 'you're a bit deep in thought.'

'How well do you know the Maxim Corporation, Brian?' Charlie asked.

'I know that they are worth a bucket load of cash to my firm,' Brian replied. 'I have heard a few things about sharp practice, but nothing too serious. Why?'

Charlie regaled Brian with the incident at Bream Bay. He also told him about Queenie's warning about bitter water and how this was the same term used by the old man at the bay.

'There are lots of references to bitter water in the Bible,' Debbie said, 'and it is a Sunday.'

'Okay you have my attention,' Charlie said, 'what point are you making?'

'Well my brother there are two things that spring to mind,' Debbie paused to ensure that she had the family's attention. 'Firstly the term bitter water or waters is used to denote evil in some shape or form.

The locals have a Christian tradition and they may be suggesting that something untoward is going on.

And of course it is Sunday, a day of rest, so let's put the subject to bed and play a game of some sort.'

'Now the schoolmarm has spoken,' Chrissie said. 'How about a game of Monopoly, New Zealand version to give us the advantage?'

Chapter 3: Summer School

It was Monday and Charlie was back in lecture mode. His first session of this busy day was a whole Summer School lecture about the various types of criminology which were emerging.

Strangely he realised that Ms Blackman's question was timely, as environmental criminology would form part of the lecture. The main point of the session was to show how the shifting face of crime was now being shaped by a changing world with technological cybercrimes and the growing harm caused by corporate crime.

'So you see that just as globalisation is shaping the world by exposing us to different cultures, so it is also leading the way in exposing people to many different forms of crime,' Charlie paused.

'So there are a series of tutorial groups which you can attend over the next two days, the list is posted at the back of the hall, and in the Summer School notes.

Thanks for your attention and I hope it was not too dry a subject. I will see you all back here on Wednesday for a riveting lecture on structure and agency as causes of crime.'

The hall burst out into spontaneous applause, which took Charlie by surprise.'

Charlie had a couple of hours before his next class, which was a session with the Law Enforcement Professionals group. The subject was to be the practical usages of geographical profiling and how to build tolerances into the findings. Charlie shuddered at the prospect, checked his pen drive contained the required presentation and settled down in front of his laptop to check emails and prepare.

There were a couple of emails from Scotland. One from Willie Noble explaining that his exploits in New Zealand with the Musket Wars had reached the papers back home. The SPA [Scottish Police Authprity] had played up their cooperation with their sister organisation is the Southern Seas, Willie said he would spare Charlie a copy of the carefully crafted prose.

Another email was from Albie Main, he and his partner were keeping an eye on Charlie's house in Cullen. All was well, and the guard dog Paco was in full voice every time Albie or Elspeth walked along the path.

Charlie took a little time to surf the web for references to Bitter Water, and found, as his sister had predicted, several hundred biblical references. He made a special check of any news items of poisoned fish or people in the Bream Bay area, but found nothing. One for Kelly's Angels he thought to himself and fired off an email asking for their help.

Almost instantly a message came back accepting the commission and promising to send the bill by return. He replied by asking the angels to split their searches between instances of pollution and research of the Maxim Corporation.

With that it was time to take to the small lecture theatre where some 40 law enforcement officers were waiting. It was amazing that they had come from all over New Zealand, from the east coast of Australia and even a small dedicated band from Hong Kong and Singapore.

On entering the lecture theatre he saw Pinkie Lumo and Kelly Browning sitting near the front which gave him an idea to liven up the topic.
Charlie proceeded for the next forty minutes to give his presentation on geographical profiling. He stopped and asked the group if anyone had any experience of using the technique. For a couple of moments no one moved or said anything, he then took the initiative.

'Okay now, I happen to know that our two students here from the local Force,' Charlie walked over to Pinkie and Kelly. 'DS Lumo and DC Browning have actually used this technique recently, perhaps they would like to share with the group the approach they took and also how successful it was?'

The pair looked horrified and shocked. Suddenly the big DS stood up and walked to the front of the room, pausing only to encourage his DC to follow him.

'Thanks Doctor Charlie,' Pinkie said, 'we would be delighted to explain.'

'Would we?' Kelly Browning said as she joined Pinkie at the lectern.
Pinkie then proceeded to draw a map on the interactive screen which was projected to the large display screen behind him, he then asked Kelly to explain the technique used to plot the events.

Charlie was very impressed by the way the pair had risen to the challenge and were making a first-rate job of explaining how they had practically used the technique.

'And to explain how accurate the results were,' Pinkie started to draw their demonstration to a close. 'The Unsub who was operating in the east of the district lived about 200 meters from the centre of the animal abuses cluster.'

Kelly Browning added, 'and the Unsub operating in the west of the district lived about 225 meters from the centre of the vandalism cluster.'
'Well thank you for that very interesting demonstration,' Charlie said, 'and do your fellow students have any questions?'

'Yes, how did you learn the technique in the first place?' a delegate from Hong Kong asked.

'Oh it was some stuffy old academic who taught it to us,' Kelly replied, 'but in the end it was a valuable thing to learn.'

The delegates sensing the joke laughed heartily.

'Of course this is just a technique and an indicator not a predictor,' Charlie said. 'As criminals become more aware of these techniques they will in some cases employ forensic countermeasures, this is part of the agency motivation of a criminal. As part of the process they make decisions on the benefits and risks.

Where a criminal is driven by structural influences, their behaviours are much less calculated and easier to predict using such techniques as geographical profiling. Remember it is a tool to be used along with other tools and skills. Thank you for your attention.'

Once the hall cleared Kelly and Pinkie approached Charlie. 'Sorry guys, but I have given that lecture lots of times,' Charlie said, 'and I saw the chance to make it real for a change. You both are naturals I was impressed with the presentation.'

'Just stuck to the facts Doc,' Pinkie said.

'So how are you doing Kelly? The musket stand-off was quite an ordeal' Charlie asked, referring to the case they had just described. 'I'm fine,' Kelly replied. 'I was scared at first but once Queenie walked into the farmhouse the fear left me. She is a remarkable old lady.'

'I know that for sure,' Charlie said. 'She has shocked me a couple of times.
So what are you guys working on now?'

'A body washed up at Peach Cove,' Pinkie replied. 'A bit gruesome as it had been in the water a while, not quite sure where the man had gone in, but we are trying to track him down.'

'So where's Peach Cove?' Charlie asked.

'It's just south of Whangarei, across from Ruakaka,' Kelly replied.

'I was at Ruakaka with your angels on Sunday,' Charlie said with some surprise. 'Just for a picnic and to give them some driving practice. There was an incident with some locals and poisoned fish.

Have there been many reports of pollution in the area?
'

'Not that I know of, Doc,' Pinkie answered. 'I can ask around when we are there next, any reason?'

'Yes, actually it's a combination of Queenie, Bitter Water and Maxim Corporation,' Charlie replied.

'A new case is it Doc?' Kelly asked.

'I hope not, just some idle curiosity,' Charlie smiled as he answered. 'Idle curiosity, yeah right, but with Queenie in the mix anything can happen,' Pinkie replied.

'Answer me this Kelly,' Charlie looked at the young DC, 'just how did Queenie get into that farmhouse?'

'Oh come on Doc have you not worked it out yet,' Kelly replied, 'she just walked in the front door.' With that she laughed and left the room.

'Thank god for that,' Charlie said, 'I thought she walked through the wall.'

Chapter 4: Maxim Corporation

Charlie had decided to return the call he had from Ms Blackman at Maxim and attend a meeting with her and Miles Anderson. So far, Kelly's angels had not come up with much on the company, only that they were an offshore company based and incorporated in New Zealand but had holdings over most of South Asia and the Pacific Islands.

'So glad you could come to meet us Dr Manson,' Ms Blackman said in an accent Charlie just could not place. 'I think we rather got off on a bad footing the other day.'

'Yes I think we did,' Charlie replied. 'I have to admit being a bit frazzled after the events of the days before. Anyway, how do you think I can be of assistance to you?'

'Well there are a couple of things Miles and I have been considering,' Ms Blackman took the lead in the conversation. 'Firstly we have a corporate dinner coming up and have been looking for an interesting guest speaker. We both thought it might be an unusual topic for our guests.'

'Have you any particular topic in mind?' Charlie asked.
'Perhaps something around your experiences with serial killers,' Anderson joined in, 'they are rather a sexy topic at the moment globally.'

'Okay, sexy serial killers, I can come up with something,' Charlie retorted, 'and what is the second thing?'

'Well that is a bit more interesting for us,' Miles Anderson explained. 'We have a group of individuals who are trying to block our developments, and well . . . we are stumped as to why.'
'You see they're trying to stop some development which would bring jobs to the area,' Ms Blackman continued. 'These are jobs that the locals badly need.'

'So how do you think I could help you?' Charlie asked curiously as to what the answer could be.

'Well you are a renowned profiler,' Blackman added, 'we thought you might be able to profile our opponents and give us some insights into how to approach them.'

'That is an interesting challenge,' Charlie said. 'To profile someone I have to have some contact or materials they have produced.'

'Yes we know you would need that and we have prepared some materials on them,' Miles Anderson replied. 'It's a combination of media footage, press releases and articles they have written. I understand that this may be tainted by the fact it is the materials we have selected but I am sure you could find other sources.'
'Just how many people are we talking about?' Charlie asked.

'There are three main organisers of the protests,' Jacqui Blackman replied.

'I am only here for another two months,' Charlie said. 'I could have a look at the materials and give you an idea if I could do the job.'

'Yes of course it would be a job,' Ms Blackman replied and pushed a pre-written cheque to Charlie with a rather large sum on it. 'We thought this would be an appropriate fee.'

Charlie looked at the cheque and nodded. 'That is quite a sum for what maybe not a great return.'

'We know it is not an exact science,' Anderson looked at Charlie, 'but we know your reputation and I am sure you will produce something of worth for us.'

'And the after-dinner speech,' Charlie said, 'that could be a donation to my sister's favourite charity.'

'Of course. Shall we say five thousand New Zealand dollars?' Ms Blackman replied.

'Sounds fair to me, I will find out what the charity is,' Charlie replied. 'I'll have a look at the materials and get back to you in a few days.'

'That would be fine,' Miles replied. 'Can we offer you a coffee or perhaps tea?'

'Actually I am fine,' Charlie said. 'I have a lecture this afternoon to get ready for.'

Charlie took his time on the drive back to the University, he was curious as to why Maxim wanted to profile their opposition. It was a normal business practice in some countries, but this set of circumstances made him cautious.

When he got back to the University he checked in with his nieces who were engaged in web searches for him.

'Hi Chrissie, how are you doing. Have you had any joy with the searches?' Charlie asked.

'Nothing yet, Charlie,' Chrissie replied. 'Gisele has been compiling some stuff on Maxim, but as to the fish situation nothing has come out.

'Okay thanks,' Charlie replied. 'Are you at any of this week's lectures?'

'Yes I will be taking in a couple,' Chrissie said, before asking 'How's Kelly doing?'

'She is fine. I think she is going to head out to see the two of you later this week,' Charlie replied.

'Great, must dash,' Chrissie replied.

Charlie decided to pay a visit to the School of Earth Sciences and check out what environmental research they do and if there was any information on Maxim. He dropped by the school's research centre and chatted with the researchers. One of whom proved to be quite informative.

'So you want to know about Maxim do you?' David Maidstone said. 'What does an eminent criminologist want with that crowd?'
'Nothing really specific at the moment,' Charlie replied. 'I'd encountered some problems with fish being poisoned down at Ruakaka and wanted to check out what Maxim did in the area.'

'Well it is nothing specific to environmental issues,' Maidstone replied. 'At the moment their base in that area is really a logistics port where goods and materials are brought in.

They are setting up some testing of shale gas drilling off the coast at Awaroa Bay on the eastern side of the peninsula. There is some local opposition, but it is just some test drilling to establish if there is any volume of gas in the area.'

'I thought shale gas was drilled for inland not out at sea,' Charlie asked. 'Is this normal?'
'You are quite right, it's normally inland areas where the gas is found,' Maidstone answered and paused before continuing. 'In this case they are looking at the shale gas being an indicator of shale oil.

That's a lighter form of crude oil that does need to be thinned down.

Find the gas and they may find the oil. The government has given them drilling rights in the sea off the peninsula, and also in the bay areas. It could mean a large sum of money for the economy, bring jobs to the area but also pollution to the environment.

New Zealanders are very cautious about pollution and the environment.'

'I see, and that has raised some protests I guess?' Charlie quizzed the researcher.

'It has within the local community,' Dr Maidstone looked concerned. 'It's also raised some hope of research funding for the Department, so tread carefully Dr Manson.'

'Thanks for the heads up,' Charlie replied.

-------- 0 --------

Charlie walked back through the campus, and arrived at the venue for his next lecture in the series at the Summer School and sat on a bench outside to take the vapours and clear his head. While he reflected on the situation, if there was one, with the offer of consultancy work from Maxim, the body off Peach Cove and a feeling that somehow they were all connected, when two tall rangy figures on racing style bikes clad in bright lycra biking gear passed him and drew to a halt.

'Charlie Manson is that you, what the devil are you doing in New Zealand?' the taller figure asked.

'Colin, Ewan I could ask you the same thing,' Charlie replied. 'Of all the green parks in the entire world you two have to cycle through mine.'

'Well we are on a charity cycle tour, bit like the one we did a few years back,' the smaller of the two replied. The size references were relative as both were well in excess of six foot tall.

'Well we retired from Police Scotland and decided to get the event out of our systems and do a cycle ride around New Zealand for charity and also as a holiday,' Colin said. 'You have still not said what you are doing here.'

'Well I am having a break, visiting my sister and her family,' Charlie replied, 'and teaching at the criminology Summer School in Auckland.'

'Doing any case work?' Ewan asked.

'Trying not to, but you know how it is,' Charlie replied with a smile. He passed them his mobile number and suggested that they get in touch to have a catch-up drink.

'Must rush,' Colin said, 'we are a bit behind schedule. The great navigator here keeps getting us lost.'

-------- 0 --------

Pinkie and Kelly were at Peach Cove; to get there meant a drive through Whangarei down some small roads and then a short walk down to the cove. There was little to be seen there, police tape surrounded the spot where the body had been found. Their interest was more in how the body had arrived there.
'We know he arrived here from the water,' Kelly said to Pinkie. 'From the description of the officers who were first on the scene it sounded like the body had been in the water for days or weeks.'

'I know, and I am not looking forward to the post-mortem,' Pinkie said. 'We have to be back at the University morgue by 4 p.m. so let's get on here.'

'We need an oceanographer, that's what we need,' Kelly stood thinking. 'There has to be someone at one of the universities in the area.

We need to know if a body would wash up here from inside the bay or out from the ocean.'

'Never mind the universities, there is the Sir Peter Blake Marine Education Centre,' Pinkie said looking at Kelly. 'Did you not go out with an ocean expert there a couple of times?'

'Well remembered you creep,' Kelly said. 'Tell you what, I will go to the post-mortem and you visit the octopus.'

'Sounds like a deal,' Pinkie replied. 'Have you any message for the octopus?'

'Yes, ask him if he has found them yet,' Kelly laughed, 'and if he has, then give him a sound kick up the nuts. It's your civic duty as an officer of the law to protect women in the community.'

'Will do,' Pinkie smiled at his partner. 'Can you remember the description of the body?'

'Yes male, bloated, greenish tinge to the skin and omitting noxious gases,' Kelly looked at Pinkie, 'a bit like my last three dates.'

'Seriously Kel,' Pinkie said.
'Yes, they reckoned he was about five foot six,' Kelly read from her notebook. 'From what they could tell, he was naturally dark skinned but not black, possibly Asian. His clothes were fair threadbare, but that could have come from immersion in the water.'

'So sounds like someone who has come off a boat maybe?' Pinkie suggested.

'Could be,' Kelly was intrigued, 'what are you thinking?'
'Nothing definite, just a thought I need to follow up on,' Pinkie said. 'Right, race you back to the car.'

Pinkie took off at speed to the car as Kelly shouted in agreement but walked. She looked down at the car keys in her hand and laughed.

-------- 0 --------

The smell in the morgue was gross, and Kelly was amazed at how Dr McCreadie worked away in these conditions. When she arrived the autopsy had already started, and what appeared to be the dead man's internal organs were in plastic containers on the side in some form of a solution.

'Glad you could join us DC Browning,' McCreadie said. 'Your colleague Pinkie would have turned green and fainted by now.'

'I know, he is off to interview a lower form of marine life at the moment,' Kelly replied. 'Anything you can say at the moment?'

'Apart from the fact he drowned,' the pathologist looked at the DC, 'not a great deal. He appears to have been in the water for some time; I would estimate weeks, perhaps three or four. Stomach contents were minimal, in fact there was next to nothing solid, mostly a pulp consistent with some form of grains or seeds. He was most certainly not local. From the bone density and musculature, I would guess Asian or perhaps from one of the Pacific islands.'
'Interesting, that's what Pinkie was thinking,' Kelly said.
'Wish he had shared his thoughts, this is one smelly corpse,' McCreadie said.

'So Doc, you would put the cause of death as drowning?' Kelly asked.

'I would indeed,' McCreadie paused and turned to the DC, 'but it is qualified by a severe blow to the back of the head perimortem, meaning just before death.

It was severe enough to fracture the skull, but not enough to cause instant death.

I would have to say that it was not caused by a blunt object but most likely a boot or big fist.

So my dear DC you have a murder victim here.'

'Oh crap, Doc' Kelly exclaimed. 'Sorry about that, last thing I would have expected, now we have to investigate this one.'

'Indeed you do,' the pathologist turned and removed his gloves. Walking over to a table where there were some remnants of clothes and a watch. These may be of some help.'

The smell of the rags of clothes was putrid; there were no distinguishing marks or labels so Kelly was prepared to leave them to dry out in the dry store used in the morgue.

The watch had been cleaned with sterile water and the residue collected for analysis, it was an expensive watch well cared for and had some writing etched on the back. The plate was worn and Kelly bagged it for the forensic team to see if they could bring out what was written on the back and any makers labels or logos which might provide a clue as to the origins.

'I've taken DNA and blood samples for analysis. We might be lucky,'

McCreadie said. 'We will hold the body in cold storage until the investigation is concluded or identifies the poor chap.'

'Thanks Doc,' Kelly replied. 'I will go and break the news back at HQ that we have a suspicious death.'

-------- 0 --------

Pinkie's trip to the Marine Education Centre yielded little information, it seemed that a body being washed up at Peach Cove would be more than likely to have come from out to sea rather than in the bay, but the expert could not be conclusive.

Kelly's expert no longer worked at the Centre. He had been let go for some administrative problems, Pinkie suspected what they had been. The person giving the advice suggested a name at Auckland University's Earth Sciences School who might be able to provide more assistance.

Pinkie decided to stop off at Auckland University to speak to the experts in the Earth Sciences School and touch base with Charlie. He found Charlie in his office.

'So, Ds Lumo, what can I do for you?' Charlie said.

'Oh just in the neighbourhood Doc and thought I would pay you a visit,' Pinkie replied. 'I also thought you might have a coffee brewing.'

'Not coffee Pinkie but tea,' Charlie said. 'Fancy a cup?'

'Very civilised tea in the afternoon,' Pinkie said. 'Don't mind if I do.'

'So how was the trip to Peach Cove?' Charlie asked.

'Fine. No way the body was dumped from inland, it looks like this is a floater who came from out at sea,' Pinkie answered. 'It looks like the body drifted in off the currents from the ocean, which means a lot of paperwork and digging to find where he came from.'

Charlie could see something was troubling Pinkie.

'So what's the problem?' Charlie said. 'Your face tells me that you are concerned about something.'

'I guess this must run in the family,' Pinkie laughed. 'I just have a funny feeling something is not quite right with this one.'

'Ah, you're Queenie's grandson right enough,' Charlie handed Pinkie his cuppa. 'So what does your gut tell you?'

'My head tells me we have not had a body wash up anywhere near there in the last 30 years at least,' Pinkie continued. 'My gut tells me bodies just don't wash up. My spirit tells me something is upsetting nature.

Kelly is at the post-mortem so we will know how he died soon, but that will just be the start.'

With that Kelly browning entered Charlie's office after knocking. 'Thought you might be here Pinkie,' Kelly said. 'About the postmortem . . .'

Pinkie interrupted her, 'It's a murder right?'

'Have you been drinking your granny's tea again or what,' she replied.

Chapter 5: Interesting turn of events

Charlie was back in his office after another lecture, he had with him a small tutorial group of law enforcement officers. They were discussing some of the more intricate aspects of serial offender behaviour. The discussion had gone beyond the standard serial killer behaviour and extended to aspects of what could be called general offenders, robbers, fraudsters and the like.

'So what you are saying, Dr Manson,' an officer from the Hong Kong police was asking, 'is that you believe that the serial behaviour so hallowed by the media in killers and rapists is also there in less violent criminals?'

'I believe it is,' Charlie replied. 'Let me explain my rather limited theory on the matter. Take a serial thief who habitually breaks into properties, is caught several times and spends a fairly long period of time, in short chunks, in prison. The act of being incarcerated has little or no effect on him. He gets out of prison, walks down a street, sees a window open and *has* to break in. He has other options, experience has taught him that this is a road back to prison, but still, he is compelled to break in.

The compulsion is the key. It is like the compulsion that a serial killer or a rapist feels. After all, rape is not about sex, it is about the abuse of power. The serial thief is not going to make much from the DVD player or few bits and pieces he nicks, it is something else that drives him in some cases, not all, I admit.

Okay, gents that's the hour up, we can pick this up next week at the same time, perhaps you can come with some ideas about how you would profile the serial thief.'

The group thanked Charlie and left to be replaced by two rather smartly dressed officers.

'Dr Manson, could we have a word,' the smaller one asked bringing out a warrant card. 'I'm DI Mitchell, and this is DS Cramer, we're from the serious frauds office.'

'Come in Gents,' Charlie replied curiously. 'What can I do for you?'

'It's a bit delicate. We understand that you have had some dealings with the Maxim Corporation,' Mitchell said, he paused before continuing, 'Ms Blackman and Mr Anderson.'

'Sit down gents,' Charlie answered. 'I've been to see them about doing some work for them.'

'Just what kind of work?' DS Cramer asked, 'if you don't mind telling us.'

'No, I have no issues with sharing,' Charlie sat back in his chair. 'They want me to profile some protestors who are opposing their developments, and also do an after-dinner speech for them.

I have to say I have no problem with the latter but have had a concern, that you two are compounding, about the former request. I take it that this corporation is of interest to the New Zealand Police in some way?'

'It is, I am afraid to say,' Mitchell continued. 'We have been interested in them for some time; they are local to the islands, and have a fairly large portfolio of investors and business associated with them.

Blackman and Anderson are just the latest in a long line of senior officers of the Corporation to have surfaced. We know that they are active in several countries in South East Asia, Australia, New Zealand and now China. The bulk of their money is held in offshore trusts so it is hard to trace its origins.'
'But you suspect organised crime as the main investors?' Charlie added.

'We do,' Cramer said. 'There's no suggestion that you're involved. I suspect that their attempt to do business with you is genuine. There is some strong opposition to their activities locally, and profiling the main players sounds a good idea.'

'So how can I help you?' Charlie knew the answer in advance of asking.

'Well we would very much like you to play along with them,' Mitchell said. 'We have tried to place someone on the inside but have had no luck so far.'

'I'm hardly on the inside' Charlie said. 'My involvement is going to be very minimal, but I can see what else they put to me, I am sure the present arrangement is just an opening gambit.'

'Yes we rather think that is as well,' Mitchell said. 'We know you have a working arrangement or contact with DS Lumo and DC Browning, we would rather like to use that as a conduit to ourselves.

I will run it past DI Goodman. Of course there is the matter of your brother-in-law Brian Wakefield.'

'What about Brian?' Charlie asked his voice hardening. 'He's not involved in anything illegal I'm sure.'

'So are we, but, 'Cramer paused looking at his partner,' we would rather he knew nothing of your involvement and our discussions.'

Charlie looked at both officers before speaking. 'Okay but if there is any risk to Brian or his business the deal is off and I tell him the lot. This is not a bargaining position it is a show stopper if you cannot agree.'

'Okay we agree,' Mitchell said, 'but should Mr Wakefield cross any lines we will deal with him swiftly.'

'Not going to happen,' Charlie snapped back.

'I hope you are right, but we are dealing with powerful criminals here,' Cramer said. 'People get tempted.'

'They do, but Brian is as honest as the day is long,' Charlie snapped back. 'Call it gut feeling but he is not the type.'

-------- 0 --------

Charlie took a trip to Auckland and walked over to Brian's office. He went into the building and was greeted by a young receptionist. 'Hello Sir, can I help you at all?' the receptionist asked.

'Yes I am looking for Mr Wakefield can you see if he is available for a few minutes?' Charlie asked. 'Tell him it is Dr Manson.'

'Oh your Brian's brother-in-law,' the receptionist was clearly impressed. 'Just take a seat he is not with a client at the moment and should be free.'

The receptionist called through and Brian came to meet Charlie straight away.

'Charlie is everything okay?' Brian asked.

'Everything is fine just thought I would catch you about something,' Charlie replied.

The pair walked into Brian's office and sat at the meeting table. 'So what can I do for you?' Brian asked.

'Brian what do you know of Maxim, Ms Blackman and Miles Anderson?' Charlie said. 'They have offered me some work and I want to know what I am dealing with.'

'What kind of work?'

'Well they have offered me an after-dinner speech job which is okay, but they also want me to profile some of the protestors to their developments, and that is the bit that concerns me.'

'I did not know about that Charlie, honestly. They wanted to be introduced to you at the dinner party but never said anything about offering you work.'

'How honest is their business Brian?' Charlie asked.

'I just don't know Charlie,' Brian slumped in his chair. 'They are very keen to get some businesses set up as holding companies and we can do that for them.

Some of the conditions they are looking for suggests that they are up to something. I have not got to the bottom of it. Have you been approached by some group about this?'

'Let's say, I can't say,' Charlie replied.

'Got it,' Brian replied. 'So I should pull out of any involvement with them?'

'Actually not yet,' Charlie replied. 'Stall them as long as you can and do the stuff you feel comfortable about.'

'Okay so you have been warned not to involve me, I get that,' Brian said. 'I can stall and do just the minimum.'
'Good well I will be off,' Charlie stood to go. 'I guess we need to keep the chat between us.'

'Agreed wild horses won't drag anything out of me,' Brian said.
'Not thinking about wild horses,' Charlie smiled.

'Or inquisitive wife either,' Brian replied, 'for the moment.'

-------- 0 --------

Charlie drove back to the campus and went to his office to find Pinkie and Kelly Browning waiting for him.

'To what do I owe this honour?' Charlie asked.

'Well it just so happens that we have been invited to meet you by the Fraud boys,' Kelly Browning said. 'They said you would explain.'

'Did they the lazy swine,' Charlie answered with a bit of a laugh.

'I see you know them by reputation,' Pinkie retorted. 'So what is the story?'

'Well I have been asked to do some work by the Maxim Corporation,' Charlie replied. 'It also seems that they are a company of interest to the serious fraud squad, who want me to fish about and use you guys as a means of feeding back to them, seeing as we are in contact a lot.'

'Okay so if you have anything we take it back to Mitchell and Cramer?' Kelly said

'Exactly,' Charlie replied, 'but I have nothing for you at the moment. What do you know about the company?'

'Very little, they're trying to expand their sites and the locals are protesting a bit,' Pinkie offered. 'We can pass anything we get to you as well.'

'Sounds a plan,' Charlie paused. 'So what are you two up to?'

'Investigating the murder of an unknown and unidentified body,' Kelly volunteered. 'That's been in the water for an unknown time and was in a really smelly condition.'

'The joys of police work,' Charlie replied. 'So that would be the Peach Cove body.'

'Yeah, but peachy it is not,' Kelly retorted.

Chapter 6: Profiles for payment

Charlie decided to look at the materials given to him by Maxim Corporation to build some outline profiles.

The three individuals were quite different. He wanted to check that nothing he supplied to Maxim would cause harm, and so spent some time watching the video materials and reading the articles accredited to the individuals. Charlie favoured the Korem Profiling technique which attempts to define an individual using their communications and performance types.

Charlie watched the video footage of speeches the trio made, and then read the articles and extracts which had been given to him for the first person. Terence Jones, twenty-five years old and a student of mathematics at Wellington University on the South Island. The technique Charlie was normally using would call for more materials and perhaps even an interview under controlled conditions, certainly a close observation of some days, but he had only the videos and the written materials to work with.

Jones came out from Charlie's analysis as an 'Artist-Conformist'.

According to Korem 'Artist-Conformist' is was one of the more unusual profiles. The subject came out as a willing follower type, not creative, in spite of the communications type being 'Artist'. His behaviour would typically be predictable and verging on fearful, the creativity he showed would be reduced with the risk factor of the situation he was in.

His writing and speeches were clever without being spectacular or innovative in their ideas. He was not a dangerous type and offered a low-risk threat to Maxim. The pen may be mightier than the sword, but the ink in Jones' pen was definitely watered down.

Charlie took a break and was joined by Dean Forrester.

'Working late Charlie,' Forrester said. 'I saw the light on.'

'Yes Dean, I kind of got caught up in something,' Charlie replied checking his watch and seeing it was 8 p.m. 'I have been asked by a business to look at some profiles for them, trying to do it out of Uni hours.'

'Not a problem, Charlie,' the Dean answered. 'Actually I had been trying to catch you to tell you the Summer School is proving a great success, in fact it will be more than breaking even. We have had a surge in late bookings following your exploits, if that's the right word, with the musket business.'

'Okay,' Charlie said, 'I will try to keep the side issues to a minimum.'
'I guess from reading the research on you,' Forrester sat down, 'this is a regular occurrence.'

'Not really, Dean,' Charlie replied suspecting there was more to this visit. 'I'm on the Home Office and Scottish Justice Department list as a forensic psychologist and criminologist, so get involved in casework.

I have a feeling, not from any profiling, that there is something on your mind.'

'Am I that obvious Dr Manson?' Forrester chuckled. 'There is something you could help us with. We have a troubled student in the School which some of the Faculty are worried about, and we wondered if you might have a word with him.'

'Troubled in what way?' Charlie quizzed the Dean.

'Well there is some talk and evidence of stalking female students,' Forrester took his time choosing his words. 'His female lecturers find him a bit difficult to reach and some are frankly quite scared to be alone with him.'
'I take it academically he is quite a high achiever?' Charlie asked.

'Very high achiever,' Forrester continued. 'In his work we can find no fault, in fact he is quite gifted. He is a top student in the undergraduate course in Criminology and Psychology.'

'Well I would be glad to chat with him,' Charlie said. 'I would like to see his record and any files you have on him first, but arrange a meeting.'

'I will ensure you get access to his record on the system,' the Dean looked relieved. 'Arranging the meeting will not be a problem. He is quite a fan and one of your Summer School students as well. His name is Mitchell Ramsay.'

'I will keep an eye out for him.' Charlie replied.

The Dean took his leave of Charlie, who went back to his task for Maxim.

The second profile was of Bruce Talbot, a twenty-nine-year-old labourer from Waipu on the North Island. His speeches had been videoed at some open events where he regularly took to the platform. His writings came from articles and letters he had sent to various local newspapers. He was clearly an intelligent man and very erudite.

Charlie profiled Talbot as a 'Sergeant/Conformist'. The type made for good second in commands, and loyal assistants. He was a man who would follow orders from one he respected. He would most likely be the group's enforcer, and highly motivated to see the group succeed.
The last of the three profiles was clearly that of the leader. Evan Newell a thirty-seven-year-old teacher from Auckland. He was originally from Australia but of New Zealander extraction. He was a charismatic orator who held a crowd with his style and content. The passion with which he spoke gave way to a lack of control and over-emotionality from time to time.

His writings at first seemed considered, but on a second review showed a surface grasp of topics. His profile came out as a 'Salesman/Random Actor'. This Charlie knew from experience meant that Newell was a threat-risk to himself, those around him and to those who opposed him.

Charlie prepared the reports on all three including how best to confront and present ideas to them, based on the technique. He looked at his watch and saw that is was 1 a.m., just enough time to get to his apartment on the campus and sleep for a couple of hours.

As he crossed the campus he came across the two ex-cops from Aberdeen, who had clearly been enjoying the wares on sale at the campus.

'Charlie working late,' Colin said. 'You should have joined us; we have been having an R&R day mostly on Limburg and Emerson beers.'

'So I see,' Charlie replied. 'Are you two heading back to the campus flats?'

'Absolutely right,' Ewan replied. 'If we can just find the right path, been trying for an hour.'

'What the great aviator means is that he is lost,' Colin replied.
'Well I am going your way, so walk with me gents and I will see you safely home,' Charlie replied.
'What about your shadow back there?' Colin asked referring to the figure that had been following Charlie since he left the block where his office was.

'I am sure he knows the way,' Charlie replied, 'but with two of Aberdeen's finest for protection I should be all right.'

'Has he been twenty yards behind you for long?' Ewan asked.
'Well,' Charlie answered 'about three days, nice to feel wanted.'

Chapter 7: Mitchell Ramsay

Charlie waited in his office for Mitchell Ramsay, the student Dean Forrester had asked him to meet, and at the duly appointed time Charlie heard a knock on the door. For some several moments before he had been aware that someone had been outside his room.

'Come in' Charlie shouted. 'Ah you must be Mitchell, nice to meet you.'

It's a pleasure to meet you too, Dr Manson,' Mitchell entered the room and held out his hand. 'I have been reading your books and papers for some time now.'

The pair shook hands, Charlie noted the young man's hand had a wet palm and there was a slight tremor denoting nervousness.

'So Mitchell, you're studying Criminology and Psychology,' Charlie tried to break the ice. 'What brought you to that subject?'
'Well I suppose it was to try to help understand myself,' Mitchell said calmly. 'I have these thoughts and do some terrible things. I wanted to know why I do them.'

Ice broken, Charlie thought, let's not get frostbite.

'So what things are those Mitchell?' Charlie asked.

'I imagine myself hurting people, women mostly,' Mitchell said, he paused to look around the room. 'And I hurt animals, mostly mice and rats. I cut them, stab them and put my fingers into their bloody wounds.'

Charlie watched the young man carefully, before speaking.
'And how does that make you feel?' Charlie asked.

'I'm disgusted with myself.'

'When, is it during the act, immediately after, or a while after?'
'Mostly a while after.'

'How do you feel before you stab the animals?'

'Aroused, excited and nervous'

'In what way nervous?'

'Oh I am not sure, just scared a bit.'

'What is causing the fear?'

'I don't know that's what I am seeking to find out.'

'So do you keep doing these things to get to the bottom of the fear?'

'That's part of it I guess.'

'How long have you felt like this?'

'As long as I can remember,' Mitchell paused. 'I think I have always had this desire to see blood.'

'How do you feel when you see your own blood?'

'Just normal sort of, it does not excite me, I sort of feel nauseous' Mitchell replied.

'Okay let's go back. You mentioned you think about hurting women,' Charlie sat forward in his chair. 'Have you ever acted on these thoughts?'
'No,' Mitchell looked at Charlie there was a flush to his skin. 'No I have never hurt anyone, not yet.'

'You say not yet,' Charlie probed the boy a bit more. 'Have you ever come close to carrying out some of these thoughts?'

'I follow women, sometimes the same one for hours sometimes many different ones,' Mitchell replied. 'That is why Dean Forrester wants me to talk to you.'

'Yes it is, he is concerned as are some of the other lecturers that you might be a risk to others or yourself,' Charlie watched for a reaction from the young man. 'What makes you choose a woman to follow?'

'Nothing special, I just get a feeling that I want to follow a person and then it starts' Mitchell replied.

'Okay, I want you to try something for me, if you are willing.'

'Okay if you think it will help,' Mitchell replied.

'Right Mitchell, I want you to sit back and relax.

Now think back to the last time you cut and stabbed an animal, I want you to think about the moments before you started.'

'Okay.'

'Now can you hear anything?' Charlie asked.

'Just the mouse squeaking a bit as I hold it.'

'How does the noise make you feel?'

'I get a bit fearful, but also excited.'
'How does it feel to you in your hand,' Charlie continued.

'It feels soft, warm and weak.'

'Can you smell anything?' Charlie continued.

'Jasmine, and musky smell of the mouse.'
'How do you feel?' Charlie asked.

'Aroused, I can feel myself becoming aroused,' Mitchell shivered.
'Anything else Mitchell?' Charlie probed.

'I can feel the fear growing,' Mitchell twitched and shuddered.

'Now what are you feeling?'

'I need to stop the feeling of arousal, so I need to strike the animal.'

'Okay Mitchell, let's go past the attack, you look down and see the mouse bleeding and cut.

How do you feel now?'

'I feel the need to clean my hands and wash the blood off.'

'And the fear and arousal Mitchell how are they now?' Charlie asked.

'They're gone; I just need to wash my hands.'

'Okay Mitchell, I want you to sit back and open your eyes,' Charlie said. 'Let go of those earlier thoughts.'

Mitchell Ramsay looked tense but started to relax, he sat for a couple of moments then spoke.
'So Dr Manson what has that session told you?' Mitchell asked.

'Quite a lot actually,' Charlie said.

'Have you seen any specialists about your thoughts?' Charlie asked.

'I am seeing a psychiatrist my parents have arranged for me,' Mitchell replied. 'They are concerned about me. Are they right to be?'

'I think you have some issues which need to be addressed,' Charlie answered. 'How long have you been seeing the Psychiatrist?'

'About six months,' Mitchell replied. 'I go twice a month.'

'What has he told you to do when you get those feelings?' Charlie asked.

'He asked me to write down what I was doing just before, and to sit and think about something else till they pass.'

'Do they pass?'

'No.'

'Mitchell do you have a girlfriend?' Charlie asked.

'No, girls find me awkward and nerdy, 'Mitchell replied. 'They find me too intense.'

'Have girls told you that?'

'No,' Mitchell replied. 'My mom tells me I am too intense and that I need to lighten up or I will never find someone.'

'Are you looking for someone Mitchell?'
'Yes I guess we are always looking for that special someone.'

'Okay that's enough for the moment,' Charlie said handing Mitchell a card with his number on it.' When you see the psychiatrist next can you ask him to call me, here is my office number.'

'I will do that,' Mitchell replied.

'Mitchell you never asked me exactly what the session told me,' Charlie said.

'Yes I think we both know what that is,' Mitchell said and left the room.

-------- 0 --------

Charlie contacted the Dean's office and arranged through his PA to meet with him urgently after his next session at the Summer School.

'So Charlie, how did you find Mitchell Ramsay?' Dean Forrester asked.

'I think you are right to be concerned Dean,' Charlie said. 'I found him to be a troubled young man.'

'How so?' Dean Forrester asked sitting down behind his desk.

'He has a fascination with blood, and admits to harming animals,' Charlie paused for a moment collecting the right words. 'He freely admits to following women, and knows that this was partly the reason why you wanted me to meet with him. He is seeing a psychiatrist and I have asked that he pass a message to the Dr asking him to contact me. Have your student welfare group had any contact with Mitchell?'

'Not really; we have a counselling service but it is voluntary,' the Dean said. 'Students have to make contact with it if they think they need help. We are considering a more proactive approach but are taking advice at the moment on how to start that.'

'Okay, I think you should ask your security staff to keep an eye on him' Charlie said.

'Do you consider him to be a risk to fellow students or staff?' Forrester asked with a degree of concern.

'I do,' Charlie looked at the Dean closely and considered his next sentence. 'He thinks he is acting out of a sense of curiosity but I think it is a compulsion.

He knows that something kicks off his actions but he claims not to know what that is.

I think he is conflicted about his sexuality and that something deep down is driving him. I am not that skilled a psychologist to give a diagnosis, but my experience with serial offenders is such that he is high risk and in need of treatment.

If I were to suggest a course of action I would suggest involving his parents, remove him from the campus for the time being and have him voluntarily admitted to a psychiatric facility for observation.'

Dean Forrester sighed. 'Actually that is the course of action I was veering towards. Certainly contacting the parents was my next task. I am a psychologist by volition and you have confirmed one or two of my suspicions but you have given me a different angle on some things. Thanks Charlie.'

'If you want me to meet with the parents as well,' Charlie offered, 'just let me know.'

'I will bring you in on that conversation,' Forrester said. 'I think first I need to have a chat with Mitchell.'

Chapter 9: Convergence

Pinkie Lumo and Kelly Browning were looking for somewhere to start to identify the body found at Peach Cove. The nature of the find and the lack of any identifying clues on the body apart from a watch left them with little or no discernible starting place.

'So, DS Lumo, where do we start?' Kelly asked her superior.

'Where would you suggest, DC Browning?' Pinkie replied.

'Dr Manson for one,' Kelly paused then continued, 'then there's Queenie for another.'

'I did suggest speaking to Charlie to the DI,' Pinkie replied. 'He suggested trying to work it out ourselves to start with, and that Charlie had been through enough. But Queenie is a possibility. First I think we need to try to set some lines of enquiry off.'

The pair cleaned off the whiteboards in their allocated incident room. It was one of the smaller rooms but still had boards on four walls and was large enough for 5 desks and computer terminals.

'So where do we start, DS Lumo?' Kelly chided her colleague.

'Well we saw Dr Manson's approach,' Pinkie replied, 'let's try that. A board for the victim, location, suspects, witnesses, motives, and Unsubs.'

'Witnesses?' Kelly asked.

'The people who found the body,' Pinkie replied. 'They were witnesses to the location and the find. They can tell us what was going on around them. We need to check the statements taken and if needs be go back and re-interview them.'

'You have been attending the lectures and taking notes,' Kelly said, 'I am impressed.'

'So impress me, Detective Constable,' Pinkie said. 'Start assembling the entries on the boards.'

'Oh I love it when you take command,' Kelly retorted. 'Now bog off and get us a couple of coffees and mine's a bacon roll.'

When Pinkie returned he was surprised to see the progress Kelly had made within thirty minutes. The information they had amassed was small but had been set out on the boards in a logical order. Kelly was seated at one of the desks reading the witness statements from the dog walker and his partner who had found the body.

'You know there is next to nothing in these statements,' Kelly said to Pinkie. 'The uniforms must have just gone through the motions.'

'To be honest Kel,' Pinkie replied, 'you saw the body. Who would have suspected blunt force trauma with that level of decomposition?'

'I guess you're right,' Browning said, 'but we have to re-interview; maybe one of those cognitive interviews Charlie lectured on.'

'Worth a try,' Lumo said continuing, 'where do we find them?'

'Near Queenie in Waipu, so two birds with one stone,' Kelly replied.
'Good idea, you drive,' Pinkie said.

-------- 0 --------

Charlie had arranged to meet with Miles Anderson and Ms Blackman from Maxim to discuss the findings of his profiling of their main protestors. He met with them at their corporate offices in Auckland, as he entered the building he could see one of the people he profiled at the main gates leading a protest group.

Bruce Talbot was standing with a small group protesting at the gates. Charlie looked the man over closely as he waited to gain entry to the grounds. The protest was well organised and orderly, no threat in their actions and they spoke with those who were entering the complex, but did not force themselves on the visitors.

As Talbot handed Charlie a leaflet spelling out the group's demands, Charlie handed his business card with his New Zealand office number on the back and said to Talbot, 'Contact me'.

Charlie had previously emailed a copy of the three reports to the pair and was going along to have a follow-up discussion.

Jacqui Blackman met Charlie in the outer reception office of the named executive suite.

'Nice to see you again Dr Manson, and thanks for the reports you emailed,' Ms Blackman led Charlie through to Miles Anderson's office. 'Miles is waiting for us.'

As they entered the large office of Miles Anderson another man was there, he was very tall, tanned and fit.

'Can I introduce Dirk Whelan to you Dr Manson,' Anderson said, 'Dirk is our Head of Security.'

Whelan introduced himself to Charlie, who straightaway detected a strong South African accent.
'Nice to meet a fellow Law Enforcement brother,' Whelan said shaking Charlie's hand. Charlie placed the man in his mid to late forties, and clearly kept himself in good shape.

'Are you ex-NIS by any chance?' Charlie asked. He was referring to the National Intelligence Service in South Africa.

'Jacqui and Miles said you were sharp,' Whelan said. 'Yes I actually predate NIS. I was employed in the old Buro vir Staatsveiligheid.

What was mistakenly called BOSS but was really the Bureau for State Security.'

'Nice to meet you,' Charlie said taking careful note of the new member of Maxim. 'So I take it you have all read the profiles of the main protestors. Is there anything I can add or any questions I can answer?'

'Your coverage of the three gentlemen matches our own evaluations,' Whelan said. 'Your suggestions for confronting and presenting to them are interesting.'

'So I take it you are planning some kind of a confrontation, or showdown with them,' Charlie asked.

'Yes, in as much as we have to take on those opposed to our plans for the area,' Ms Blackman was at pains to play down the confrontation. 'Clearly the confrontation will be peaceful and geared at persuasion.'

'So what exactly are the plans that they oppose?' Charlie asked.

'Well they have a bee in their collective bonnets about the potential fracking off the coast for one thing,' Ms Blackman said, adding 'and there are objections to the developments at our Northport base.'
'Northport is a logistics point for us, you understand,' Miles Anderson was quick to jump in.' We need a sound base to bring in plant and equipment and that is what the base there gives us.'
'I take it you are bringing in that plant and equipment from China and South Korea?' Charlie asked.

'Well assumed Dr Manson,' Whelan added. 'You have done some homework.'

'Well I like to know who it is I am doing business with,' Charlie paused. 'I mean the Maxim Corporation is one that has heavily been invested by South African interests.

I guess that's where your involvement comes from Mr Whelan.'

'It does I am here to ensure the operation is secure,' Whelan paused. 'And the interests of our principles are maintained.'

'I see, making sure their investments are secure,' Charlie added. 'Well are there any questions for me?'

'Not really Dr Manson, we may have some more profiles or a bit deeper analysis of these ones for you,' Whelan said, clearly he was leading the conversation for Maxim. 'We know where to find you.'

'I'm sure you do Mr Whelan,' Charlie smiled. 'I take it your man who has been following me for the last few days.'

'Consider him removed,' Whelan said. 'You passed the test.'
'Thank you.'
-------- 0 --------
Charlie sat back in his office looking at a map of the seas between China and New Zealand pondering what it was that needed a secure base at Northport. The routes he could see passed by Vietnam, Philippines, Malaysia, Indonesia and Papua New Guinea. He made a list of the countries on a whiteboard under the heading of Maxim Corporation.
He sat looking at the board as Pinkie and Kelly came into his office.

'Oh guys good to see you, I need you to get some information to Cramer and Mitchell,' Charlie said. 'Mind you, rather you than me.'
'So Doc what's this about?' Kelly asked.

'Oh it's just a list of countries that the Maxim Corporation's ships must pass,' Charlie said. 'They head down to Northport to deliver plant and equipment I am told.'

'Doc can I make a coffee,' Kelly asked. 'Anyone else wants one?'
'Help yourself,' Charlie answered. 'Mine is white with a sweetener.'

Pinkie Lumo stood staring at the whiteboard and pulled out his notebook, looking through the pages and clearly making some mental connections.

'You know this might be the answer,' Pinkie said.

'Okay but what's the question?' Charlie joked, then looked at the board himself.

'Peach Cove,' Pinkie answered. 'Kelly what was it Doc McCreadie said about our body, he could be Polynesian or Asian.'

Kelly Browning looked around at the boards with the countries listed, she gave a whistle.

'Are you thinking this guy came off one of Maxim's boats?' Kelly asked.

'Yes,' Pinkie said, 'and technically they would be ships. Doc Charlie, it's possible right?'

'Yes it's possible,' Pinkie can you get details of the passage of ships in the area?' Charlie asked.
'Yes we can,' Pinkie replied. 'The Ports Authority requires notice of passage and also the ships will have an itinerary registered.'

'So it's smuggling of what,' Kelly asked, 'people, drugs or something else?'

'Absolutely it's smuggling of something,' Charlie answered, 'but precisely what, that's the question.'

Maxim is supposedly a wealthy company, so why would they be smuggling, what is the most valuable cargo to smuggle into New Zealand that might come from those countries?'

'Drugs, guns, people,' Pinkie said, 'it could be any of these.'

-------- 0 --------

Pinkie made contact back at HQ with DI Mitchell. He explained the conclusion that Pinkie, Kelly and Charlie had come to as well as the possibility that the body at Peach Cove was linked to Maxim.

DI Goodman joined the pair. 'So Pinkie you suspect that your case and the DI's here are linked?'

'Yes Boss,' Pinkie said. 'It does seem to be something of a coincidence the route that Maxim's ships take and the body.

I spoke to some marine experts who said that a body could not have landed on the cove where it did coming from the bay, it most likely had to be from out at sea.'

'DI Mitchell have your investigations into Maxim suggested smuggling?' Goodman asked. 'I thought it was more environmental crimes that they were under investigation for.'
'Well to be honest,' Mitchell replied. 'We were at a bit of a loss to know what they were up to and smuggling fits as well as anything else.

What we need to do now is get some information on the routes taken by the Maxim ships and anything else that docked at Northport.'

'I think it might be worth a surveillance crew keeping the port under observation,' Goodman said. 'Pinkie get on to the team and have them set something up.

How did you come to the connection?'

'Doc Charlie worked some of it out,' Pinkie replied.

'Charlie's in on this too,' Goodman said.

'Yes' both Pinkie and DI Mitchell replied.

'I thought he was here for a break,' Goodman laughed.

-------- 0 --------

Charlie decided to drive out to his sister's place to touch base with his family. On the drive out he was pondering the connections between Maxim and the body at Peach Cove. He knew that whatever it was it was most likely illegal, he was also waiting for contact from Bruce Talbot.

'Charlie how are you?' Debbie said as he entered the house. 'Chrissie has been trying to contact you the last two days.'

'Oh I have not checked my emails I guess,' Charlie said absent-mindedly. 'I've been caught up with Pinkie and Kelly on a case.'

'A case?' Debbie said with a large note of surprise, 'again.'

'Yes well it started with contact with the Maxim Corporation,' Charlie explained. 'That has led to a body in Peach Cove, dumped off a boat. That looks like it ties into smuggling, and from there who knows.'

'You best speak to Chrissie and then Brian,' Debbie said, 'they're linked as well I think.'

Charlie approached the dining room where his niece Chrissie was busy on her laptop surfing the web.

'So there you are Charlie,' Chrissie said seeing her uncle.' I've been trying to get hold of you. I have some background information on Maxim.'

Chrissie went on to explain that there were many postings on websites about the Maxim business model. Most companies were linked to Maxim by franchise or licensing agreement to use their software or name. The company had a huge range of subsidiaries and from her web search she found that in many countries the business practices of Maxim were considered to be dubious or questionable.

Chrissie handed over a pen drive to Charlie containing a wide range of data, reports and downloaded articles all categorised and recorded in an index.

'Very impressive Chrissie,' Charlie noted. 'You could get a job at the Police out of this.'

'Dad is already talking about a little part-time job with his firm as a researcher,' Chrissie said with a smile. 'The sticking point is the money, I am holding out for a better rate.'

'Your mother's daughter,' Charlie replied. 'So where's your Dad?'

'He's out in the garden by the summer house,' Chrissie replied.

Charlie went out to see Brian, who promptly explained that his firm had dropped their interests in Maxim following a discussion with the partners; he could do little to stall the change in policy.

'Any special reason?' Charlie asked.

'Yes Arnold Taylor the senior partner was on a trip to Oz and came back with some interesting gossip,' Brian replied. 'We checked it out and found out it is not exactly gossip but evidence of some sharp practices.'

'Yes, Chrissie has just been giving me her findings,' Charlie said. 'I will be checking it out later.'

'Good and wait till you hear from Gisele on Maxim,' Brian said, 'she has a different angle again.'

Gisele explained to Charlie that she had been in contact with friends who live near the Northport depot and they had told her security had been increased, and that people were being chased away on a regular basis.

Charlie left the Wakefield's home with much food for thought, as well as a very enjoyable dinner.

Chapter 10: Meetings and Invitations

Charlie was sitting back in his office at the University after his first session at the Summer School. The Summer School was a mixture of lectures, seminars and workshops. Charlie was enjoying his time presenting and working with groups of participants who came from a variety of backgrounds. Some were students, both undergraduates and postgraduates who were taking the chance to mix with seasoned law enforcement professionals from a wide range of locations in the southern seas.

This morning's session involved Charlie giving a lecture on interview techniques, and then handing over to staff from the University who were holding a series of workshops where the participants would get a chance to try out some new techniques. He was sitting looking at the whiteboards which held details of the Maxim Corporation and the Peach Cove case when there was a knock on the door.

'Come in,' Charlie shouted as he rose to greet the visitor.

'Dr Manson,' Bruce Talbot entered the office. 'You handed me your business card the other day and asked me to contact you.'

'Yes, Mr Talbot please come in,' Charlie said extending a friendly hand which the visitor shook with a strong firm grip while fixing Charlie with a curious stare. 'I guess you are wondering how I know your name.'

'Yes I'm curious as to why a Professor in Criminology would want me to make contact' Talbot said.

'Take a seat please. Can I get you a coffee or tea?' Charlie asked, while assessing the man as they spoke.

'Tea would be fine,' Talbot replied, 'black no sugar.'
'Well, I was asked by a local company to profile you and a couple of your colleagues,' Charlie explained as he made the pot of tea.

'I am sure you can work out who they are, and now that I have completed the work and learnt a bit more about them, I am curious to know why you are protesting against them.'

'Thanks for your candour,' Talbot replied. 'They are a bit of a sham organisation. They claim to be environmentally friendly and working with local communities, but in reality their activities are suspect.
Take the shale gas and oil drilling off the spit at Ruakaka for instance, the question no one has asked is "What oil and gas?".

There is no evidence to suggest there is any, apart from the survey that Maxim claims to have carried out.'

Charlie handed Talbot his cup of tea, 'So are you saying there is no gas or oil in that area?'

'Speak to any of the experts in the field and they will tell you the chances of any finds there are limited,' Talbot became quite animated. 'For there to have been shale gas or oil there needs to have been a history of forestation or vegetation dating back thousands of years.

The geological history of that area is of a coastal nature. The drilling is bogus, and the security so strong that only from the air can you see anything, and even then it is a picture of going through the motions.'

'So what do you think is going on there?' Charlie asked.
'I don't know for sure,' Talbot sounded frustrated. 'It's a front for something else. That's the way Maxim's franchises operate.'

'I take it you have evidence of this,' Charlie said hoping to verify Chrissie's finding. 'Surely in the test drilling for gas there was some government approval?'
'Look at their activities in Australia around the Perth coastal drillings, there are the same claims,' Talbot pulled out some papers from his jacket and handed them to Charlie. 'Claims of shale gas and oil but after extensive drilling nothing found.'

Charlie looked at the cuttings and papers, which backed up Chrissie's findings.

'So Bruce,' Charlie handed back the materials to Talbot. 'What do you think is behind this? To set up bogus drilling like this takes some cash.'

'I've no idea what they are up to,' Talbot sounded frustrated. 'Eco Watch Angels, the group I am part of, have tried to find out with requests through the Official Information Act, like your Freedom of Information Act in the UK, and so far nothing.

As to the cash side of it, whatever it is, it has to be serious enough to merit the expenditure and that means illegal and valuable.'
'I agree,' Charlie said, 'that normally means drugs, guns or people. I don't think there is a huge market for guns in New Zealand, so unless they are using New Zealand as a staging post to somewhere else it is unlikely to be guns.

Smuggling drugs is the most likely, but you cannot rule out people trafficking. More money can be made through drugs, but again New Zealand does not have a massive population so the market is limited.'

'The population is just under five million, about the size of Scotland,' Talbot said, 'and we suspect people trafficking.'

'Has your group any hard evidence?' Charlie asked.

'No, we have not been able to get too close to the drilling site or to the Northport depot,' Talbot replied. 'I take it you're investigating this on behalf of the Police?'

'No, not yet,' Charlie said. 'Just curious and putting some facts together.'

'You sound like you will be working with the Police,' Talbot sounded a curious note.

'Just a gut feeling that's all,' Charlie laughed. 'Can I ask that you contact me if you find out anything, and I will do the same? Can you leave me a mobile number it will stay between us?'

'Sure, I think you're honest enough,' Talbot replied writing his mobile number down on a piece of paper on the table. 'I'll take my leave of you now. Thanks for the tea.'

'No charge for the tea,' Charlie said as Talbot walked towards the door, something in his stance gave Charlie an idea. 'So Bruce, do you need a copy of my schedule for the next few days or will you just be following me blindly.'

'Ah, thought you spotted me the other day,' Talbot sounded sheepish. 'We had to be sure about you once we saw you were linked to Maxim, and by the way there was someone else from Maxim on your tail.'

'I know, I thought you were them,' Charlie said,' can I take it the following stops now?'

'Yes, consider it done.'

-------- 0 --------

Pinkie sat in the interview room reviewing the evidence he had so far on the Peach Cove John Doe body. His focus was on the information they had on the passage of ships associated with Maxim and their contacts with the islands en route from China and locations in the areas off New Zealand. Kelly Browning was busy on her laptop checking out the pattern that was on the back of the watch taken from the victim.

'So what have we got?' Pinkie said out loud. 'The possibility that the body came off a boat from the fleet that Maxim run. The possibility our body comes from one of the islands or countries that are along the route. The possibility that this ties into people trafficking, or drugs, or guns.

What we have are a whole lot of possibilities,' his frustration clear to be heard.

'Do we have a docking in Malaysia?' Kelly asked.

'Three in total,' Pinkie replied. 'Why?'

'Because that's where the watch came from,' Kelly printed the details and took them over to the DS.

Pinkie reviewed the printout, and looked at the port docking and the timeline. He identified two potential boats that the victim may have come off. One docked at Northport.

'The Ptarmigan looks most likely,' Pinkie sounded suddenly lifted by the information. 'Kelly get on to the Port Authority, see if you can trace where the ship is now. I need to speak to the DI.'

'Oh yes sir your magnificence,' Kelly strode off to see what she could find.
-------- 0 --------
'So DS Lumo you think the boat this victim came off was the Ptarmigan,' Goodman said, 'and you think the evidence is strong enough for us to search it?'

'Yes, it looks a good bet to me,' Pinkie said. 'I am sure there might be evidence still on board if we can get there.'

'We have to hope it is still in New Zealand waters,' Goodman said. 'By the way I have asked MacKinnon and he agrees we should ask Charlie Manson into the investigation. Are you okay with that?'
'That's more than okay, boss,' Pinkie said. 'Shall I ask him or will you?'

'I'll take care of that, you track down the ship.'

-------- 0 --------

Dean Forrester knocked and entered Charlie's office. 'Dr Manson, Charlie glad I caught you,' the Dean looked a bit more relaxed than the last time he had seen Charlie. 'I have some news on Mitchell Ramsay.'

'Come in Dean, can I get you a coffee or tea?' Charlie asked.
'No thanks I have to rush off,' Forrester replied. 'I just wanted to let you know that Ramsay has agreed to be sectioned.

I spoke with his parents; they were extremely concerned and have been for some time. They are travelling in Australia at the moment, but I spoke with them at length and they agreed along with Mitchell that he should submit himself to a spell in a psychiatric facility. He went in this morning.'

'Glad to hear that, Dean,' Charlie said, adding 'he is a very troubled lad and it's the best place for him.'

'Right, I must be off,' Dean Forrester said as he left Charlie's office, just as DI Barry Goodman was entering.

'Barry, nice to see you, what can I do for you?' Charlie asked.

'Well Charlie I need to ask you a favour,' Goodman entered and sat down. 'I need to ask you to help out with the Peach Cove case.'
'Okay glad you asked, as I think it is related to something I have been working on,' Charlie replied.

Charlie explained about the contact he had with the Maxim Corporation and how he was sure they were connected to the body washed up at Peach Cove.

'Pinkie and Kelly will try to meet with you here, save you travelling all the time,' Goodman said. 'But you will need to be handy for briefing and case conferences.

Charlie, I have to explain the reason for asking you in. The local government in the area have put pressure on to get a resolution. The body that washed up is clearly not a native of New Zealand, so there is some political pressure to find out where it originated.'

'I understand,' Charlie said. 'Barry do Maxim have any political clout around here?'

'They do Charlie,' Goodman answered, 'it's very subtle at the moment. They are potentially going to bring jobs to the area, and that is a major prize.'

'So the politicians might have turned a blind eye to the planning requests?' Charlie asked.

'It's a possibility for sure,' Goodman replied. 'The thing is, it's one that would be hard to prove.'
'I'll touch base with Pinkie and Kelly,' Charlie paused. 'Barry, Maxim wanted me to profile some of their opposition, I did so. I have just met one of the people I profiled and to be honest he was hiding something.

I will pass the names to your DS and DC to have a dig into.'
'Got a funny feeling about the guy, Charlie?' Goodman asked.

'Let's just call it an old coppers nose,' Charlie replied.

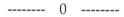

-------- 0 --------

The next day Charlie attended a case conference that had been convened by Barry Goodman. When Charlie entered the room he could see that Barry was less than happy about something. DS Lumo, DC Browning, DI Mitchell and some others Charlie didn't know were present.

Goodman called the meeting to order.

'Okay, let's get started folks, we have quite a bit to cover,' Goodman sounded very business-like. 'Now for the purposes of the Peach Cove investigation DS Lumo is going to act as the primary investigating officer. What we thought was a simple case of a drowned body turning up on the beach at Peach Cove has now become a murder investigation. DS Lumo can you explain how this turned into a murder investigation.'

Pinkie Lumo gave a presentation on the facts as they had developed including a description of the post-mortem report.

Charlie took over from Pinkie with a presentation showing the sailing routes of Maxim ships and the potential ports that the victim could have boarded from. He also explained that Maxim was interested in profiling their opposition.
'We need to get some surveillance at the Northport depot,' Pinkie said. 'Does anyone know the area?'

'I do and it will not be easy,' answered a uniformed officer. 'They have a fairly open space all-round the depot with little cover for surveillance to be mounted from. It will be hard.'

'A visit to the site by officers will no doubt alert suspicion,' Charlie said. 'I have an idea. Let me speak to a couple of people I might be able to get someone to have a recce.'

'Okay Charlie,' Pinkie said, 'it sounds intriguing.
What we need to do is covertly build a picture of Maxim's activities and do a bit more research on the company. DI Mitchell, is this one where you can provide more intel for the next briefing?'

'It is,' Mitchell replied.

'Okay let's meet tomorrow at 4 p.m. does that suit everyone?' Goodman asked.

As everyone agreed the briefing closed.

Chapter 11: A pair of lost cyclists

'So let's get this straight,' Ewan asked, 'you want me to get both of us lost deliberately in the Northport depot so we can snoop for you on this case?'

'Yes,' Charlie answered. 'I want you to get in there, pretend to be lost and see what there is to be seen.'

'Gawd, with him navigating pretending will be the hard bit,' Colin said before going on to ask. 'And we are looking for something out of the ordinary?'

'Yes, we cannot get a surveillance team nearby because of the terrain,' Charlie replied. 'But a couple of experienced officers with first-rate observations skills wearing cycling lycra is a perfect disguise.

We know that they are up to something at that depot, but cannot get close enough to see what it is. The complex is well protected, we know that, and it is situated in such a way that it is hard to see much.'

The two retired officers looked at each other and then at Charlie. 'We'll do it,' Colin said, 'retirement is not all it's cracked up to be.'

The two retired officers went with Charlie to a special case conference in HQ. Charlie introduced them, and Pinkie Lumo went on to explain their role to the team.

'Colin and Ewan will make their way into the complex on the pretence of being lost,' Pinkie explained. 'While on the site they will have a good look around for any signs of unusual activity.'
'I'm sure with the brightly coloured cycling gear,' Goodman interjected, 'you guys will take them by surprise.'
'Can I ask a question?' a young PC asked.

'Certainly PC Taylor,' Pinkie replied. 'What is it you want to know?'

'Just how tall are you?' he said to Colin.

'I am six-foot-eight,' Colin replied, 'the tallest retired cop in Scotland.'

The group broke out into a round of laughter.

'Okay guys a bit of decorum here please,' Pinkie said, 'these two gents are taking a bit of a risk to help us out here.

Sergeant Gallagher will brief you on the complex and the roads,' Barry Goodman said.

Goodman and Pinkie walked over to Charlie.

'I have to say, Doc,' Pinkie looked at Charlie, since you have been here we have got into a couple of different situations, but two guys over six-foot tall, in pink and green cycling lycra is something I never thought I would see in a briefing.'

'Well Pinkie they're bloody good cops,' Charlie looked at the pair standing being briefed on the site they were to go into. 'Police Scotland let a lot of talented coppers go and these are two of the best, mind you their dress sense has kind of gone off a bit.'

-------- 0 --------

Pinkie travelled with Colin and Ewan to within a few miles of the Northport deport in an unmarked van that was big enough to hold their bikes and some limited radio surveillance kit.

'Okay guys Northport is just ten kilometres down 15A you cannot miss it,' Pinkie said.

'You hear that,' Colin said. 'Pinkie said we cannot miss it, I would not bet on it with him navigating.' He looked at his colleague Ewan and shook his head.

'Honestly guys, it's a straight road,' Pinkie said. 'Well it's not straight but just follow the signs if you go more than ten kilometres you'll have have missed it.

The Maxim dock is at the end of the road, don't take any risks.' 'We may be pensioners technically,' Ewan said, 'but we have all our marbles.'

'Okay good luck,' Pinkie replied. 'I'll be waiting here and listening. Remember you say "looks like Peterhead" and I will be down that road sirens blaring.'

There's a checkpoint at the entrance to the depot and we know they have guns, so be careful.'

'We'll just tag behind a lorry going through and head in,' Ewan said.

The pair made their way down 15A. It did not take them long to reach the entrance to the Maxim docking area, and as luck would have it the barriers were up to allow a lorry to enter the complex, the pair tailgated their way through security into the complex.

'Hey you two stop or we will shoot,' the guard shouted after the pair of cyclists, 'I mean it.'

Colin and Ewan ground to a halt, looking round in all directions taking in as much of the interior of the depot as possible for the benefit of the micro cameras attached to their cycling helmets.

'Very sorry,' Ewan said, 'he's inclined to get us lost from time to time,' nodding in Colin's direction.

'I get us lost,' Colin reacted, 'now there's a novelty.' What about that time at the Falkirk wheel when you went the wrong way?'

The pair continued to argue and look around them as the guards approached.

'Gentlemen you must leave the complex at once,' the lead guard said, 'this is private property.'

'I don't suppose you have a dunny I can use,' Colin asked spotting an open shed just twenty yards to the left of where they were standing. 'Is there one in there? Pee yourself in these shorts and it can be a bit obvious.' He motioned to move to the shed as one of the guards rushed to stop him.

'Not in their mate,' the guard replied, 'try over there where it says *Gents.*'

'Sorry about that, never saw it,' Colin said quickly. 'You know the sight of automatic weapons like that can make a man want to go.' As Colin engaged the guards Ewan looked closely at the open shed and could see some movement in the doorway.

On his return from the gents Colin tried to questions the guards. 'Guys that' a lot of firepower to protect a wood loading dock.' He pointed at the weapons.

'Well that's just company policy,' the main guard replied. 'So if you would like to leave the complex we will have no reason to use them.'

The pair left, but took with them digital recordings of the site and the surroundings which would help the Police plan their next moves.

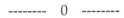

-------- 0 --------

Back in the incident room in Police Headquarters, Pinkie, Kelly, Charlie, Barry Goodman and the two undercover cyclists reviewed the video evidence.

'This is a great boost,' Goodman said, 'when did you get the idea?'

'We have had the cameras on the helmets for ages,' Ewan explained. 'Part of the charity fund-raising was to post footage on Facebook.'

'We just thought it was worth the risk,' Colin added. 'We just thought we might get something.'

'Well it looks like we have something,' Charlie said. 'There is something in that shed that they do not want anyone to see. And as for protecting the site with automatic weapons, what is that all about.'

'Normally it would be illegal, it's only collectors that are allowed to hold them,' Goodman replied, 'and even then, they have to be disabled.

I have checked and Maxim employs a security firm who are licensed by the Government to hold the weapons.'

'Boss, surely the way they were presenting them at Ewan and Colin was against the spirit of the law?' Kelly Browning added. 'It's worth checking out.'

'Okay Kelly,' Goodman replied, 'that's your next task.'
'I could not be sure, but I think voices were coming from that shed,' Colin added. 'They sounded foreign.'

'That's right,' Ewan added. 'I could not make out the language but it was not English.'

Charlie pondered the still image of the shed and walked away from the desk thinking.

'So Charlie what's on your mind?' Goodman asked.

'What kind of people do you need to keep others from seeing,' Charlie replied, adding, 'in a shed under armed guard.'

'People you are trafficking illegally,' Colin added.

'Spot on,' Charlie said. 'Is there a market for that kind of trafficking in New Zealand?'

'No not here,' Pinkie added, 'but in nearby countries there could be.'

'And I guess that would explain the interest of Mitchell and Cramer,' Charlie said. 'I never really bought into the business scams angle.'

'Well we have traced the watch our John Doe was wearing to Malaysia,' Kelly added.

'There is a points scheme in place and 750 people are allowed in each year from countries mandated by the UN,' Goodman said. 'There are also about 650 allowed in from the Polynesian agreements. Malaysia is not one of those countries.'

'So that could be it,' Charlie said. 'But would Maxim take that kind of risk for the return? Just doesn't make sense.'

Chapter 12: Uncovering Meaning and Motives

'Pinkie did you ever find out what Queenie meant when she talked about *Bitter Water*?' Charlie asked.
'No Charlie, I never asked her,' Pinkie replied. 'Could it be important?'

'It may be, she seemed quite definite about the term,' Charlie replied. 'Perhaps it's worth a visit.'

'Well let's take that trip,' Kelly said. 'We need a breakthrough and Queenie has her ways.'

-------- 0 --------

'Doctor Charlie and Kelly come in and take a seat,' Queenie said. 'Grandson, go and make some tea for my guests.'

'You're welcome Granny nice to see you,' Pinkie said following his instructions.

'How can Queenie help you?' Queenie said.

'Queenie when you were at the party at my sister's you said something about the lady who was introduced to me,' Charlie looked at the old lady. 'What did you mean by Bitter Water? Has it something to do with what her company is doing off the coast?'

'It does now Doctor Charlie,' Queenie answered sitting closer to Charlie. Now what do you know of the history of the forcing of peoples of colour to go to other lands?'

'Not a great deal of detail Queenie,' Charlie replied. 'I know of the slave trade and the horrible conditions that slaves endured and their loss of identity.'
'Well some ships stopped the slave ships,' Queenie closed her eyes as if she saw something else. 'They blocked the passage and the Royal Navy of your country sent ships from the *Preventive Squadron* to intercept the slave boats.

Sweet Water and Bitter.'

'It's a book,' Pinkie said coming through from the kitchen. 'I gave you for your Christmas a year or two ago, Granny.'

'That's right boy, a sad powerful story,' Queenie said. 'But the British, like Charlie, came and stopped the trade in people of colour.'

'Queenie, how does Ms Blackman tie into this?' Charlie asked.

'Well now Doctor Charlie, you know that Queenie knows things,' the old lady smiled at Charlie. 'She is told things by people and she knows what they mean.

This lady she knows about the boats they are her boats and she brings people here to do menial things. She brings slaves to Aotearoa.'

'What are the slaves brought here for?' Charlie asked.

'Not for here, but through here,' Queenie said. 'Now Ms Kelly I want you to go and stand outside. Take my Grandson with you. Queenie has to tell Charlie something that is not for your ears.'

Kelly and Pinkie did as they were told. Once they left Queenie moved closer to Charlie and said in a quiet low voice.

'Them slaves are made to do dirty things, Doctor Charlie,' Queenie closed her eyes and shook her head. 'Things that no one should be made to do, you know, Doctor Charlie.'
'I know Queenie, thank you,' Charlie said.

'But, Charlie, the lady she is not all bad,' Queenie said, 'she is in between a rock and another rock.

People in this are not what they seem, you have to tread carefully and see the true nature of people.

Now go and get them innocent young people back in to have their tea.'

-------- 0 --------

'So spill what's the big secret?' Kelly said to Charlie as they drove back to HQ. 'Is it something juicy?'

'No, she was just protecting you young innocents,' Charlie said with a big laugh. 'She told me that this has to do with trafficking sex slaves.'

'My grandma told you that,' Pinkie said.

'She did, and before you ask,' Charlie replied, 'I didn't ask how she knows.'

'So you think this is about smuggling people for the sex trade?' Kelly asked. 'Because our body at Peach Cove was not what you would say likely to fit that trade.'

'I know Kelly,' Charlie replied 'so we have a mixture of smuggling going on I suspect.'

'Where do we start with this?' Pinkie asked. 'I mean it's a new area for me.'

'With the nagging doubts,' Charlie said to the DS, 'with the nagging doubts.'

Chapter 13: Shocking discoveries

Charlie got a text from Pinkie asking him to contact him as soon as he could.

'Pinkie what's so urgent?' Charlie asked when Pinkie replied to his call.

'Thanks for making contact,' Pinkie replied, he sounded stressed.'

We are out at Whangarei Heads further round the coast from Peach Cove. There's been a find, it's worse than Peach Cove.'
'In what way?' Charlie asked.

'We have eight bodies, male and females,' Pinkie said. 'They have been in the water for a while, not a pretty sight. Bodies never are, but these are bad.'

'Do they look like they came off a boat?' Charlie asked.
'Hard to tell, certainly looks similar,' Pinkie sounded breathless.
'What can I do for you?' Charlie asked.'

'Can you meet us at HQ,' Pinkie replied. There was the sound of much activity in the background. 'Barry Goodman wants to kick this up a notch and would like your input.'

'Sure thing,' Charlie replied, 'I will be there in an hour or so.'

-------- 0 --------

Charlie was horrified when he saw the video footage of the site where the bodies were found. The still images of some of the bodies showed clear signs of gunshot wounds. It looked like these people had been murdered then dumped off a ship.

'Okay so this finding is a game changer,' Barry Goodman said as he watched the footage. 'We are dealing with not just a random dumping of a body but some kind of mass murder.'

'These bodies look like they have been in the water for a while,' Charlie said. 'Has the pathologist given any idea?'

'Dr McCreadie reckons at least a week,' Pinkie said. 'It appears that the warmer waters down that coast speed up the effects of water on the bodies. He also said that at least six of the victims were shot, small calibre weapon he thought, but will know more after the post-mortems.'

'We have a media blackout for the next 48 hours,' Goodman noted. 'The local press and nationals have given us that amount of time to establish some facts.

The Commissioner has pulled some strings, but he also wants answers.'

'Charlie, have you come across this kind of thing before?' Kelly Browning asked her voice cracking with emotion.

'Not this,' Charlie replied. 'This is not your average murder, if there is such a thing.'

'Where do we start with this?' Pinkie asked.

'Well you start with the victims,' Charlie replied. 'Victimology is the key, who are they, where did they come from, what were they doing and what happened to them? Find out about them and you can tell a lot about the killer.'

'Is this connected to Maxim?' Kelly Browning asked. 'I mean we thought the first body was linked, but now we have eight more. Why would a company like them be involved with something like this?'

'Very good question,' Goodman said. 'We need to go at them hard, any thoughts Charlie?'

'Yes I have,' Charlie sounded angry. Something in what he had seen had hit him hard. 'They wanted me to profile some of their opposition, which I did, and to be honest something never quite squared with the profiles and the materials they collected. I think maybe I need to spend some time profiling them.'

'What can we do in the meantime?' Pinkie asked.

'Well, let's look at the main players; did anything come up on the names of the three people they had me profile?' Charlie asked.

'Nothing yet but I will get the crime analysts to put a rush on it,' Goodman replied.

'Then I think we also need some checks on Blackman and Anderson,' Charlie continued. 'Barry what do you know of DI Mitchell and DS Cramer?'

'Interesting question Charlie,' Goodman replied. 'Why are you interested in them?'

'Call it intuition or nagging doubts,' Charlie replied, 'something is not quite right there and I cannot put my finger on what it is.'

'Okay I will tackle digging into these two,' Goodman answered. 'If anything goes wrong with that it is down to me. Pinkie and Kelly you take the others and chase up the analysts on the three targets from Maxim.

The clock is ticking on the black out so we have to move fast.'

-------- 0 --------

Charlie sat down to recall his discussions with MS Blackman and Miles Anderson to try to build a picture of them. It was a difficult prospect as he had fairly limited contact with them, and did not want to make contact at the moment until the rest of the investigation had made some inroads.

His only option was to make contact with his brother-in-law Brian, as he had been dealing with the pair for some time on the legal work Maxim wanted Brian's firm to take on board. So a trip to visit the family was required.

'So mid-week and a visit,' Debbie said. 'What brings this on, a case perhaps?'

'You should have been a cop,' Charlie joked.

'No, one is enough in the family,' Debbie laughed.' Besides which, most of my family seem to be unpaid researchers for you, so who are you after now – my husband?'

'Right again,' Charlie said, 'I need a chat with Brian.'

'He is in his study,' Debbie replied. 'Dinner will be ready in an hour so make it quick.'

Charlie knocked on the study door and entered, Brian Wakefield was engrossed in some web searches and Charlie could see the Maxim company logo on the screen.

'Charlie good to see you,' Brian said. 'What can I do for you?'

Looking at the screen Charlie replied, 'I suspect you are doing it already, I need to chat with you about Ms Blackman and Mr Anderson, if you have a minute.'
'I think we have about sixty minutes before we get the call,' Brian replied checking his watch. 'What's up?'

Charlie explained about the kind of bodies and the latest developments in the case involving Maxim he was assisting on. This included the media blackout which Charlie was at pains to stress. He explained that he needed to understand a bit more about the pair, and as Brian had a fair amount of contact with them he might be able to help Charlie build a profile.

'Okay Charlie what do I have to do?' Brian asked.

'Well I need you to answer four questions about each person,' Charlie explained. 'It's called the Korem technique. I use it as a preferred method of profiling. From the answers to the questions it would give me an idea of how to approach and confront them.'

'You are planning to confront them?'

'Well, it would give the Police a method of approach,' Charlie replied.

'Sometimes Charlie you sound like you wish you were back in uniform.'

'I do I guess,' Charlie replied, 'but I'm happy to help from the sidelines.'

'Yes sidelines,' Brian laughed, 'like in a farmyard facing an armed lunatic.'

'You sound like your wife.'

'Now that's below the belt Charlie,' Brian smiled as he replied. 'So let's get to it before the bloodhound shouts us through for dinner.

So how does this work?'

'Well there are four questions, two relating to communication style,' Charlie explained. 'From those we determine types for both and then putting them together we get a profile type.
Ready, let's start with Miles Anderson.'

'Okay, fire away.'

'Does he ask what you think or tell you what he thinks when he communicates?' Charlie asked.

'He tells you, for sure.'

'Good, does he control or express his emotions when he communicates?'

'Controls 100%'

'Right. Now his behavioural type. Is he confident or fearful when making decisions?'

'Very confident,' Brian replied.

'Finally, is he predictable or unpredictable?'

Brian thought for a few moments before saying, 'Predictable, I would say from what I have seen, there are no surprises.'

'Good, now for Ms Blackman,' Charlie said. 'Ask or tell?'

'She is one who asks,' Brian said, 'it's very much a case of what do you think about this or that.'

'Control or express emotions?'

'Very controlled,' Brian replied.

'Fearful or confident?'

'I would say fearful when in Miles' company,' Brian said. 'She defers to him when a question is put with comments like "Don't you think so Miles?".

She doesn't give you a direct reply or opinion when he's about.'

'And finally, predictable or unpredictable?' Charlie asked.

'Now this is tricky,' Brian replied. 'I would say predictable, she never says anything that comes as a great surprise.'

'Great,' Charlie made careful notes of the answers. 'Now, Dirk Whelan?'

'Whelan,' Brian looked puzzled, 'I've not heard of him, where does he fit in all this?'

'Ah that's a good question,' Charlie answered, 'I'm beginning to wonder about that myself.'

'So what do the profiles tell you?'

'I need to think them through a bit Brian,' Charlie answered, 'but there are no random actors. That's a good thing. We should be able to plan strategies to handle them.'

'DINNER'S ready,' Debbie shouted.
The two men left the study at once not wishing to be sent to bed without their supper.

 -------- 0 --------

Talk over dinner was much about this latest case, Debbie was not amused.

'So what's the case about this time Charlie?' Chrissie asked.

'Well to be honest we don't know yet,' Charlie replied. 'It is some kind of smuggling but we are not sure what is being smuggled.'

'Charlie, remind me what you came over for?' Debbie prompted.

'See the family, lecture a bit and have a break. It seems to have turned into a busman's holiday.'

'I know things have just worked out this way,' Charlie replied, 'but I promise not to get caught up in anything else after this.'

'Yeah well seeing is believing,' Debbie replied with a laugh. 'You Charlie Manson can't help yourself. Some interesting case comes along and you're hooked. Now eat up.'

'So, Uncle Charlie, anything in it for Kelly's Angels?' Gisele asked.

'Actually, you could do some research,' he paused to check his sister's reaction, 'on Eco-Watch Angels, I have never heard of them before.'

'We are on the case,' Chrissie replied.

'Here we go again,' Debbie said as she went to fetch the next course of dinner.

Chapter 14: An opening in the case

Pinkie and Kelly Browning were busy in the incident room. They had been checking various reports from the crime analysts that had been requested and searching criminal records for information.

'Pinkie, Brian Talbot should only be about three years old,' Kelly said, 'according to the information available on him.'

'What are you on about?' Pinkie replied.

'There is nothing on him from longer than three years ago,' she replied. 'There are just no records from before then. He has not paid tax or anything.'

Pinkie looked over Kelly's findings and the reports from the analysts. 'What about Evan Newell and Terrance Jones?' Pinkie asked.

'Jones' academic record and career seem genuine,' Kelly continued, 'but Newell is like Talbot. There is nothing before three years back, they're ghosts.'

Pinkie started checking the reports he had been looking at, he sat back in his chair scratched his head and said, 'That's interesting; Maxim has only been active here for four years. So it appears those two appeared a year after Maxim.'

'It sounds like some kind of undercover operation?' Kelly asked. 'Looks like it, but who runs an operation for three years like this?' Pinkie asked not expecting an answer. 'Think we need to speak to the boss and Charlie.'

 -------- 0 --------

Pinkie and Kelly were in Barry Goodman's office when Charlie arrived, they had called him with their news.

'Okay so what we have are two of the three people Maxim wanted to be profiled having no record of any sort before three years ago,' Goodman said. 'What else do we know?'

'Well we know that they have no tax records until they surfaced three years back,' Kelly said. 'Interestingly there are no employment records before then either.

There were no passports before then, and there are birth certificates for both; we are still checking death records, as you suggested, Charlie.'

'If they are some kind of security services,' Charlie said, 'then making these checks will raise a few flags.

What about Mitchell and Cramer, Barry, has anything popped up about them?'

'Nothing yet, I have tapped into a few sources and eyebrows raised,' Goodman replied. 'I'm more worried about these two mystery men.'

'Well Kelly's Angels are checking out their organisation,' Charlie said. 'I think it is time to have another word with Talbot.'
'Sounds like a plan,' Goodman replied. 'What has the pathologist said about the bodies found on the coast?'

'Nothing yet, he's our next port of call,' Pinkie said, adding 'when will the press embargo break?'

'Tomorrow evening,' Goodman replied. 'The Force press office is going into overdrive trying to control the media. The Commissioner and Justice Minister will both be makings statements and be aware they are pushing for a breakthrough.'

'We need to get a case conference together as soon as possible,' Goodman said. 'I have made the request for more officers and your involvement will be made formal Charlie, in case any legal actions are coming out of this.'

'You said in case, boss,' Pinkie said. 'Do you have some doubts?'
'We have to be realistic,' Goodman stood and walked around his desk. 'If this is some kind of secret or covert operation we may be told to stand down, and we would have to comply.'

'So we have to push ahead as fast as we can before then,' Charlie interjected.

'Too bloody right,' Goodman sounded focused. 'If we can get ahead of the game then it will be hard to hide anything.'

-------- 0 --------

Barry Goodman called in some favours he had outstanding with people within the Ministry of Justice. Some people he had been at the Police Training College with had risen up the ranks and moved across to the administrative side of policing. He discovered that Mitchell and Cramer were part of a special investigative unit geared towards investigating corporate crimes, although Mitchell had a reputation of being a bit of a loose cannon.

He made contact with an old friend who worked for the New Zealand Security Intelligence Service, who promised to get back to him.
Barry spent the rest of the morning making calls and thinking about the situation. What he could not understand is why Mitchell and Cramer had approached Charlie before they had contacted the local Force. Sitting a few miles away in his office at the University, Charlie was having the same thoughts.

Charlie's method had always been to logically list and draw out the elements of a case, find headings and work through the situation. He was busy musing over the names of Mitchell and Cramer along with the three protestors he had been asked to profile, wondering what connected them all. His thinking was broken by a phone call.

'Charlie, its Kelly Angels here,' both girls could be heard on speaker phone from their end. Chrissie sounded buoyant on the phone. 'We have done the research and it's quite interesting.'

'Okay Angels, give me your news,' Charlie said his mind thinking back to the old TV series.

'Well Eco-Watch Angels are little more than a group on Facebook,' Chrissie explained. 'They are a closed group you have to ask to join. We haven't done that yet in case they get suspicious.

Looking at the postings that are public it seems to be all general stuff that you find on many Ecology and environmental group sites.

The thing is that on some of the more established groups sites there are comments about Eco-Watch that suggest people are suspicious about what they are. Some postings suggest they're a bit of a shady Government group, which the Ministry of the Environment has quite vehemently denied.'

'That's great, you two,' Charlie said, 'you'll need to come to the UK to help me out there occasionally.'

'Well actually, Uncle Charlie,' Gisele said, 'we want to talk to you about that next time you're here.'

'Okay we'll talk,' Charlie said, 'after you have spoken to your parents.'

'Spoilsport,' Chrissie said.

Charlie ended the call and made notes on his whiteboard. He looked at the boards for a few minutes and then left to attend to his next lecture at the Summer School.

-------- 0 --------

Pinkie and Kelly were not enjoying their trip to see Dr McCreadie, the State Pathologist. The post-mortem on the bodies found at the coast was not the best way to spend a morning. McCreadie had called in help from two other pathologists, one of whom had flown up from the South Island.

'DS Lumo, I have to thank you for the practice,' McCreadie said jokingly, 'but please stop finding bodies for a while, or at least not ones that have been in the sea for this long.'

'I'll try Doc,' Pinkie replied trying to keep his mouth and nose covered. 'Anything you can tell us?'

I think it is fair to say the bodies have been in the water for at least four weeks,' the pathologist stated. 'Add to that they've all suffered gunshot wounds to the back of the head, even the two children.'
'Execution style?' Kelly asked.

'Yes, DC Browning,' McCreadie added. 'I would say these were executions. You are looking for someone with a nine-millimetre weapon.
I have sent two bullet fragments for analysis and you may get a weapon type if you are lucky.

I can also tell you that these bodies appear to come from the same location as your Peach Cove body.'

'Could they be related, Doc?' Pinkie asked.

'I would guess the same boat,' McCreadie replied. 'And before you ask, we are sending DNA for analysis so we will be able to tell if they are related biologically.'

'The dental work on some of these bodies is interesting,' Dr Crawford the pathologist from Wellington said. 'It is relatively recent and fairly high end, that may give you a clue or two to track down.'

'How recent?' Kelly asked.

'I would say within the last six months,' Crawford replied he continued pointing to two bodies on tables covered by green surgical sheets. 'On the two younger ladies over there it was very extensive and costly. One of them had also had rhinoplasty, a nose job, and the other breast implants the serial numbers on the implants may lead you to the doctor who performed the surgery.'

'That's great, finally a break,' Pinkie replied.

'Might I say, DS Lumo,' Crawford cautioned, 'backstreet work will be hard to trace, the dental work is high end but any bloody fool with a knife can implant silicone. The serial numbers are on that pad there for you.'

'So they were investments in the sex trade,' Kelly said.
'Yes Kelly,' Pinkie added, 'and someone blew away the investment; that will cause a few ripples.'

-------- 0 --------

When Kelly and Pinkie Lumo reported to the briefing the results of the post-mortems on the latest bodies there was a buzz around the room.

'Okay settle down,' Goodman said to the case team which had now grown significantly. 'As you can see we finally have some solid investigative leads which may take us a bit further down the route to identifying the victims and hopefully that will lead us to the killers.

After this briefing we will split out some teams to track down the serial numbers on the breast implant. Once we have that it will be a case of trying to tie that back to some of Maxim's ships and ports they docked in. We know that the watch from the original victim at Peace Cove came from Malaysia. With any luck we can narrow the port down.'

Goodman nodded to Pinkie who took over the briefing.

'Right, now the media embargo is over. The press and TV news channels are now reporting on the find, it's vital that we control the information that goes out, so any requests you get from the media should be passed to the press office,' Pinkie paused before continuing. 'And keep the pillow talk to a minimum, we know what happened recently, and that cannot happen again.'

'Will the information about the breast implants and the search be released?' a uniformed officer asked.

'No, that is to be kept quiet for the moment,' Pinkie replied. 'It gives us a chance of getting closer to the Unsubs, so we need to use the information carefully.'
'Now as you can see Dr Manson is here,' Goodman added. 'He has joined the investigation team again, for the time being, that is also to be kept under wraps.

He will be doing some work that we need to keep away from Maxim and the Eco-Watch protest group. Charlie would you like to explain about the protestors and the profiles Maxim asked for.'

'Nice to be in front of you again,' Charlie opened his part of the briefing before continuing. 'I was asked by the management at Maxim to profile some of their protestors using video footage and printed materials.

The profiles were not very informative, but a trace on the people they wanted to be profiled was.

Terrance Jones is an academic at the University here in Auckland and appears to be who he presents himself to be.

Brian Talbot and Evan Newell on the other hand don't appear to exist before three years ago; they are clearly working for some kind of organisation which as yet is unknown. Traces are ongoing to find out who these people are, their photos are on the screen and details about them are in the information packs that have been circulated.'

With that he handed back the briefing to Barry Goodman.

'Okay we need to get some more information on these two ghosts,' Goodman explained, 'and as with the previous bits of information not for discussion outside this room and certainly not with the press.

Sergeant Gallagher will hand out your assignments, the DC's group will get theirs from DS Lumo, as I said we are finally making some progress let's keep at it now.'

The briefing was relatively short but with the leads that had been established there was much to progress.

Chapter 15: Confronting the usual suspects

Charlie attended the Maxim clients' dinner as guest speaker. This was his first contact with Blackman and Anderson since he delivered the profiles and also since the news broke about the bodies discovered at Whangarei Heads coast.

'So are you ready to wow us?' Ms Blackman said to Charlie when she met him as he entered the dining room.

'I hope so,' Charlie replied. 'I would not want your guests to fall asleep in their starters.'

'No, that would not do at all,' Blackman joked, 'but I am sure that is not likely to happen. Are you involved in the case of those bodies that have been found?'

'Why,' Charlie replied, 'are you?'

Ms Blackman looked visibly flustered and seemed at a loss for a reply as Miles Anderson joined the pair.

'Nice to see you Dr Manson,' Miles Anderson said. 'Terrible business that find of bodies up the coast isn't it?'

'Yes it is,' Charlie replied, 'must be really bad for the people trading business?'

Anderson's eyes narrowed and then regained their normal appearance. 'Is that what the Police suspect?'

'Yes it is,' Charlie looked at both his hosts before continuing.

'Actually it looks like the victims were being trafficked for the sex trade.'

'Victims?' Ms Blackman said.

'Yes victims,' Charlie answered in a low voice, 'well where I come from that's what you call someone who has had a bullet through the back of the head.'

'So we can take it you are working with the Police on this,' Miles Anderson said, 'it must be an interesting case for a visiting professor.'

'You can take from that what you will,' Charlie looked directly at Anderson. 'I am interested in any case where there are innocent victims murdered for profit.'

'Migrant sex workers are hardly innocent,' Anderson retorted, 'they are in a very dangerous trade.'

'Migrant sex workers,' Charlie said, 'it's interesting that you use the word *migrant*. Begs the question as to who was transporting them. I do not see the interesting Mr Whelan. Will he be at the dinner?'

'No, he has had to attend to some urgent business,' Anderson replied. 'Shall we take our seats?'

-------- 0 --------

Pinkie and Kelly were busy with a team of officers calling around the various manufacturers of implants to try and identify the source of the one recovered from one of the victims.

'This will take days. How many manufacturers are there?' Kelly asked.

'Not sure, but the serial number must mean something to someone,' Pinkie replied. 'It's the best lead we have.'
'I never thought there were as many medical suppliers and surgeons as this in New Zealand,' Kelly replied.

'I know,' Pinkie replied, 'we need to Kelly's Angels, but I suspect the topic would not be approved of.'

'No, but we don't need them, we need to use their method,' Kelly said. 'They think out of the box and link searches on the web through search engines, I have seen them at work.'

'Meaning?' Pinkie asked.

'We search with the serial numbers and other terms', Kelly replied. 'For example, use the serial number and the term PIP for Poly Implant Prothèse. That's a type that is banned in most countries but maybe not where the work was done.'

'We could search for clinics along the likely path of the ships,' Pinkie said.

'Now you are thinking out of the box,' Kelly answered.

The pair stopped the officers who were searching and explained the approach to be taken. Within an hour they had a result.

'Boss,' a uniform shouted from a terminal at the far side of the incident room, 'I've got a hit.'

Pinkie and Kelly walked over to the officer.

'The Durva Clinic in Batu Pahat was supplied with that particular serial number,' the officer explained. 'I got a hit on the supplier and emailed them for details of the unit they sold.'
'Great work,' Pinkie said. 'Now we need to get details from the hospital or clinic then tie it to a person.

Okay folks thanks for the efforts, DC Jones here will stay with us and we will take it from here.'

The remaining trio started to track down the patient involved.

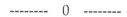

-------- 0 --------

Barry Goodman took the call from DS Lumo to tell him about the breakthrough, he was glad to hear that some progress was being made. His round of calls to various agencies had so far shown little return.

A knock on his door brought a break to Goodman's chasing up of contacts, 'Come in,' he shouted.

'Sounding a bit fraught there Barry,' Graham Standish said as he entered the office, 'how the devil are you?'

'All the better for seeing you Graham,' Goodman replied. 'What brings you to my door I wonder?'

'Wonder no more my friend,' Standish said. 'You have raised a bit of a stink with your investigation into Talbot and Newell. You have raised so much of a stink that I am here to find out what you are after.'

'So what can the Ministry of Foreign Affairs and Trade tell me about these two?' Goodman asked. 'I take it you are still with that department.'

'I'm still there and well let's say I have been asked by an international group to have a word,' Standish walked over to Goodman's desk and pulled up a chair. 'These two are working for some of our international partners and have been working on an investigation of Maxim for a couple of years.'

'A couple of years,' Goodman sounded surprised. 'That's a serious investigation, what are they looking for?'

'It's all a bit need to know,' Standish replied, 'but I know you have nine bodies and that does make it need to know. As you may have suspected it has to do with people trafficking and especially people for the sex trade.'

'Charlie Manson hit on that first,' Goodman said. 'Why is it taking two years to get beyond the investigation stage?'

'Yes, Dr Manson, I will get to him later.' Standish continued, 'Well it's not a straightforward investigation, we are talking several different countries all with different takes on human rights and people trafficking. Had it been drugs related we could have shut them down by now.'

'So is this where you tell me to stand down?' Goodman asked. 'It will take a bit to get the Force to forget about nine bodies.'

'Now Barry, would I do that to you,' Standish replied with a smile on his face. 'Don't answer that.

No, I am here to propose that the international group can help you bring some justice to the victims.'

'At what cost?' Goodman asked. 'This sounds like a bit of a forerunner to something I am not going to like.'

'Been a cop far too long, Barry,' Standish retorted. 'No tricks; the international group needs a local Force to do the arrests and prosecutions. Once you have them and they have been through the courts, our international partners can follow up.'

'And just where does Dr Manson come into this?' Goodman asked.

'Well we would like him to do some of his magic for us,' Standish replied.

'Your international partners must surely have their own resource,' Goodman paused for a bit before continuing. 'So why Charlie?'

'Well our partners tell us that he has tweaked Maxim's interest,' Standish winked at Goodman, 'and that's in a way that could be helpful.

Can you arrange a meeting?'

'I'll see what I can do,' Goodman replied. 'Now how do you and your international partners propose to help my investigation?'

-------- 0 --------

Pinkie and Kelly waited as the DC who connected the victim to a hospital followed up trying to identify the patient involved. They busied themselves by looking at shipping records to trace ships operated or leased by Maxim and the ports nearby the hospital, in all there were ten possibilities. They tried to narrow the field.

After some discussion and conferring with DI Goodman they set about contacting the ships to check on passenger manifests, this might tip Maxim off but it was agreed that this might be the best option. Barry Goodman was yet to share the information he had obtained from Standish, he decided to wait for a while before making it widely known that 'international' authorities were involved in an investigation.

Charlie had completed his after-dinner speech for Maxim, took the generous applause and bid his goodbyes to Ms Blackman and Miles Anderson. He sensed in Blackman regret or anxiety about the situation and knew that she may be the one to break ranks at Maxim. In Miles Anderson he sensed a hardness of purpose which spoke of his compliance with the business area Maxim had strayed into. For Charlie, the question was why should a company with a global presence such as Maxim get involved with people trafficking and the sex trade? As the investigation started to move forward there were still many unanswered questions, but the breakthrough to gain answers was not far away.

Instead of returning to the accommodation the University provided him while he was at the Summer School, Charlie returned to his campus office, poured himself a generous Islay malt whisky, and studied his wallboards. He was looking for connections, links and inspiration. As the liquid warmed the back of his throat, he sat and pondered the events, and information which had been shared. A knock came to the door.

'Come in,' Charlie said.

'My, I think I need you on the Faculty full-time,' Dean Forrester said, 'thought only I worked these late hours.'

'Well not University work really, Dean,' Charlie replied, 'it's a consulting case again.'
'Guess the trip is not working out as restful as you hoped,' Forrester looked at the glass Charlie had in his hand.'

'Help yourself, Dean,' Charlie replied. 'No one should be without a wee dram.'
'You're quite right Charlie, and it's Alf,' Forrester said. 'Dean is only during the hours of daylight. You look like you have a real problem here.'

'Aye Alf,' Charlie replied. 'It might be a two or three-dram problem.'

'I've been trying to catch you anyway,' Alf Forrester said. 'I have some news on Mitchell Ramsay. His parents have taken him back to Australia to a secure mental unit there. The advice from the place he submitted to here was not very good.'

'He is a very troubled lad,' Charlie replied. 'I think it is for the best. I never really had too much time to do a full appraisal but he worried me.'

'Well what you did confirms my fears,' Forrester paused, 'I think he has a long road back to mental health if it's at all possible.

Now what do you have here, I take it that this is connected to the bodies found off the coast?'

'It is,' Charlie stood up, walked over a poured himself another dram, offering a top up to the Dean who nodded his agreement. 'There is just something not adding up, all the ducks are in a row but it's just not right.'

'Maybe a fresh start another day will bring some clarity to the picture,' Alf replied.

'You could well be right,' Charlie paused. 'What do you know of the Maxim Corporation Alf?'

'Not a great deal,' Alf Forrester replied. 'They took over a local environmental outfit that was going nowhere, can't remember the name but they were near going bust.

Suddenly Maxim came in and picked them up. It all came as a bit of a surprise.'

'Well that's news,' Charlie said, 'opens up another line of why. Thanks Alf.'

Chapter 16: Visitors

Charlie was back in his office his one lecture of the day's Summer School completed, he was however nursing a small hangover. Dean Alf Forrester had stayed for a while the night before and had left by taxi shortly after midnight. Charlie looked at the empty bottle of malt whisky and understood the hangover.

The morning lecture had gone well, he was on autopilot for part of it, but the students attending the Summer School were all very engaged with the event. Charlie made himself a strong cup of tea and sat at his desk reviewing the group submission from one of his classes when there was a knock at the door.

'Excuse me are you Doctor Charlie?' a young native boy asked.
'I'm Dr Manson yes, can I help you?' Charlie asked.

'I will get the lady,' the young boy replied, 'please to be staying here.'
Charlie laughed to himself at the young lad and did as he had been told, waited for the lady to arrive. He was shocked to see Queenie entering his office; he immediately shot to his feet and came to help her to an easy chair.

'Queenie I am honoured to have you visit me,' Charlie said. 'Would you like a cup of tea, it is freshly made?'

'That would be very nice Doctor Charlie,' Queenie replied looking around the office, 'are all these your books?'

'No they belong to the Professor who normally uses this office,' Charlie replied. 'Now what brings you to see me?'

'Well I know from my grandson that you're helping out on this case of the bodies found off the coast,' Queenie replied. She paused to sip her tea and then continued, 'I know that there are some bad men at the back of this that the government man wants to catch, but you are a good man Charlie Manson. That your heart is good and you want to help the poor people who are being killed. The man from the government will let them die to catch his prey, but you will help the people first. '

'Are you saying that there is a man from the government who is letting people die, Queenie?' Charlie looked at the wise old lady. 'Do you know his name?'

'I don't know his name, but he uses ships to trap the bad man,' Queenie became very serious,' and the bad men kill them people rather than be found out. You have to stop them some other way. You must find the man who is bringing the people to Aotearoa before he kills more.'

'Why is he killing them?' Charlie asked. 'Is there something you know?'
'I know there is a powerful lot of learning in these books,' Queenie replied as she pointed at the full bookcases, but Queenie knows about the Sweet and Bitter water.'

'What does that mean?'

'Well the people from your land used to try and stop the slave trade', Queenie said calmly. 'It's in the book Pinkie gave me, the sweet and bitter water were the boats that tried to catch the slavers, but when the slave boat captains see them coming they killed the slaves and throws them overboard so they cannot be arrested.'

'So you are saying the government man knows which boats have people on them? 'Charlie asked.

'Oh yes,' Queenie took Charlie's hand. 'You must show this man you know the names of the boats too, make him stop.'

'I'll do what I can, Queenie,' Charlie replied.

'That's good now Queenie must go back home,' the old lady stood and shook Charlie's hand. 'The boy outside get him to come in and help Queenie, she has been away from her home too long, and thank you for the tea. You must come to my home before you head back to Cullen.'

'I will Queenie, and thanks to you,' with that Charlie opened the office door and the young boy came and took Queenie by the arm and led her away.

-------- 0 --------

Charlie settled back to digest Queenie's information and make some sense of it when there was another knock on the door.

Ewan and Colin the two retired cops from Aberdeen came into see him.

'How are you doing Charlie,' Colin asked. 'Are you in need of a couple of handsome retired cops in Lycra to do some more undercover work for you?'

'Not quite yet, but maybe soon,' Charlie replied. 'I take it you two are having a rest day.'
'Yes, we decided to have a day off and come and see you,' Ewan said. 'How's the case going?'

'Ah the truth comes out,' Charlie laughed. 'You're having withdrawals from work.'

'Something like that,' Colin said, 'so how's the case going, spill the beans.'

'You see it all,' Charlie replied pointing to the whiteboards. 'We are somewhat stuck. There are now an additional eight bodies and it looks like it's a people trafficking case, tied to the Maxim Corporation, but keep that to yourselves.'

'Begs the question why,' Ewan said. 'Why a company like that ties itself into this kind of trade, surely they are making money through their legitimate activities?'

'Yes that is something I am curious about as well,' Charlie added. 'It seems they bought up a local business that was hitting the skids probably for that depot at Northport. But why this kind of dirty work.'

'Well you know the old adage, follow the money,' Colin said. 'That would be my line of investigation.'

'Sounds like a plan,' Charlie answered. 'I wonder what kind of takeover it was back then.'
'How did the bodies found end up on the coast?' Ewan asked.

'Well as it is you two,' Charlie replied. 'They were shot and dumped overboard from a ship of some kind, and they drifted ashore at the east coast of the headland.'
'Shot?' Colin said.

'Aye, back of the head, execution style,' Charlie said, 'all eight, including two kids.'
'We saw guns on the guards at the depot,' Ewan added, 'but not nine-millimetre stuff, this was automatic weapons.'

Why kill them?' Colin asked, 'Seems a bit extreme.'

'Well I have it on good authority,' Charlie paused for effect, 'that it was to get rid of the evidence of trafficking before some ships were boarded.'

'Where did you get that?' Colin asked.

'You're not going to believe it,' Charlie replied, 'but Pinkie Lumo's granny.'

'Really?' Colin said, 'and what is it with the nickname?'

'I have not had the nerve to ask, and yep his granny,' Charlie laughed and continued. 'She helped break the last case I got involved with, the Musket war thing.'

'Grannies, muskets and bodies up the coast,' Ewan said, 'makes Aberdeen look tame; bet you cannot wait to get home.'

'Anyway, if you need us,' Colin said, 'as long as there are nae guns, give us a shout.'
With that the pair left and Charlie went back to his musing. Then there was a knock at the
door . . . .

-------- 0 --------

'Come in, Charlie's emporium never closes,' Charlie exclaimed. To his surprise, Kelly, Pinkie and Barry Goodman came into his office.

'Tea and coffee are over there, whisky is in the wooden cabinet,' Charlie said greeting his visitors. Now what can I do for you all?'

'Sounds like we have come at a bad time,' Goodman said apologetically.
'No not at all,' Charlie smiled, 'forgive me you are my third group of visitors today, and it is still not lunchtime.'

'So been popular this morning?' Pinkie joked.

'Yes, Pinkie Lumo,' Charlie retorted. 'It all started with a wise old lady you are well acquainted with.'

'Who Doc?' Pinkie asked than added, 'Not Queenie.'

'Yes, Queenie,' Charlie replied as Pinkie fell back on a chair.

'You are kidding me,' Pinkie said. 'She never leaves Waipu. When she came to your sister's dinner party it almost took a sedative to get her calm on the journey.'

'Well she was here.' Charlie said, less than an hour ago brought here by some young boys who treated her like royalty.

Then I had Colin and Ewan the Lycra undercover men and now the local Force's finest.'

'Are you sure you would not prefer us to come back another time?' Goodman asked.
'No, Barry, ignore me,' Charlie replied. 'I am just a tad hung-over due to last night's visitor, Alf.'

'Alf?' Kelly asked.

'Dean Forrester to you Miss,' Charlie joked. 'Okay what can I do for you?'

'Well, we thought we could go over the recent developments with you,' Goodman explained. 'And see what you made of them; maybe even come up with some ideas for moving forward.'

'Okay shoot,' Charlie said. 'But do it quietly.'

Goodman explained with the help of Pinkie and Kelly the progress that had been made.

Firstly Kelly outlined the tracing of the implant to a hospital, and how they were working to track down the patient. Pinkie told Charlie that investigations were being made as to which ship was involved, but they were a little away from naming the ship, but progress was being made.

Barry Goodman enlightened the three others as to his conversation with Standish. Pinkie and Kelly were shocked that Goodman had not explained this before now, but kept their surprise to themselves.

'So just which agency does Standish claim is involved?' Charlie asked.

'He was non-specific,' Goodman replied. 'I suspect Interpol or some United Nations based agency.
I understand he wants to meet you about some profiling, and has asked me to facilitate this.'

'Okay, that's interesting,' Charlie said with an air of caution. 'I really need to check back with the Scottish Justice Ministry and SPA about the protocol involved with dealings with an international group, especially an unidentified one.'

'So what's in the partnership working for us,' Charlie said, 'well you, oh you know what I mean.'

'Information about the ships involved I suspect,' Goodman answered. 'But then, if we come by that information on our own that is a game changer. The international agency wants us to make arrests and lead on the prosecutions, which I take with a huge pinch of salt.'

'So I am a bit lost,' Kelly interjected. 'This international agency has been working on Maxim for several years. They know something about the activity that has brought about nine deaths and yet they have not given us the information.

Something is wrong here; surely they should be on our side.'

'Kelly, they are on their own side,' Pinkie replied. 'Never forget they are more political than police.'

'Cynical my good DS,' Charlie said, 'but sadly true.

Now as to the deaths, well that's where your grandma comes into this. She explained what she thinks has happened.'

Charlie went on to explain the role of the Sweet and Bitter water ships in the slave trade and how slavers killed and dumped their human cargo to avoid detection and arrest, and how this seemed to be the case here.

'Does she know anything for sure?' Goodman asked.

'I don't know,' Charlie replied, 'but she has an insight into stuff around here that is uncanny.'

'Pinkie your thoughts?' Goodman asked.

'I would put nothing past her, boss,' Pinkie replied. 'She gets the information from somewhere, I have never found out where.'

'So what are we saying, Standish is trying to cover his arse?' Goodman asked. 'To be honest, it sounded like that when I met him, slimy git.'

'Boss, I am shocked,' Kelly joked.

'Then you must have lead a sheltered life,' Goodman replied with a laugh, 'and that's not the canteen gossip.'

'Please don't tell,' Charlie could not contain himself, 'till my hangover is gone.'
'Okay so what's the plan?' Pinkie asked.

'We keep pushing to identify the patient and the ship,' Goodman said. 'We string Standish along to get what we can out of him, but it would be good to throw the names at him before he offers them.'

'I will meet with him,' Charlie said. 'Let me see what he is made of'.

'You plan to profile the man who wants you to profile someone else?' Kelly asked.

'Yes,' Charlie said with a smile.

'Think we best clear out his booze,' Kelly retorted, 'he's gonna need a clear head.'

'Very funny, Miss Browning,' Charlie continued, 'there is more here.

Alf Forrester knew a bit of the history of Maxim in New Zealand and suggested that we check out the purchase of the company who owned Northport; he thought there might be some questionable dealings involved.

And my two former colleagues from Aberdeen suggested following the money, which ties in.'

'Anything left for us to do, Doc?' Pinkie said.

'Yes, close the door and pull the do not disturb sign as you leave,' Charlie shot back.

'We will,' Goodman said. 'And I will advise Standish you will meet him, just not today.'

'Fine.'

-------- 0 -------

After the officers left Charlie resumed his reading and thinking about the case. Maxim as an organisation still troubled him.

Then there was a knock at the door.......

'Come in,' Charlie shouted with an air of resignation that his day was not going to be his own to control.

'Dr Manson, sorry to disturb you, but could I have a word?' Ms Blackman said as she entered the office.

'Certainly,' Charlie replied. 'Now you were the last person I expected.'
'Are you expecting someone else?' Ms Blackman asked, looking somewhat puzzled. 'I can come back another time.'

'No, forgive me,' Charlie smiled. 'It's just that I have had a stream or river of visitors today, all unexpected, and I was sure there would be more. You were just not on the mental list I had just compiled. What can I do for you?'

'Well I am not really sure, it's delicate, and perhaps it's a mistake,' Blackman was struggling for words.

'I have not seen you at a loss for words before,' Charlie said, pausing for a moment, so let me try to help out here.

If you want to know what the investigation into the bodies found up the coast is I can't tell you.

But if you have come to tell me something about what you know of the situation, well I can listen, but my advice will be that you need to speak to the Police.'

'It's actually more of a question,' Ms Blackman continued. 'If I were to come forward with some information that may be helpful, would it help with any penalty I may face for my involvement?'

'It could not hurt that situation,' Charlie was curious. 'It would depend on the level of your involvement.'

'I suspect that I would need to have a lawyer present,' she smiled, 'and not your brother-in-law.'

'Brian would be more than capable of helping you I am sure,' Charlie replied, 'but no, perhaps it would be best to have someone else.'

'That's what I thought,' Ms Blackman looked nervous and concerned. 'Thanks Charlie for the advice. I will go and find a lawyer and head off to the Police station.'

'You're welcome.'

Ms Blackman left Charlie's office, he was none the wiser as to just what she would have to tell the Police, but he was sure it would be a significant input to the investigation. He called and reported the visit to Pinkie Lumo straight away.

Then he waited for the next knock on the door.

None came.

Chapter 17: Consequences and surprises

Pinkie took a call from the incident room and putting the phone down he called Kelly Browning to come with him, they had a report of a suspicious death.

'So we have a car accident that has been cited as a suspicious death,' Kelly said as they drove towards the scene.

'How does that even compute, accident *and* suspicious?'

'Guess we will find out when we get there DC Browning,' Pinkie replied. 'Get out of the wrong side of the bed this morning did we?'

'No we did not, DS Lumo,' Kelly fired back. 'And I guess we will see when we get there.'

It took the pair about 20 minutes to get to the scene of the accident. It had occurred on a notorious stretch of road which had been the scene of several accidents in the past which made the pair even more curious. When they arrived at the scene the location had been taped off, the corner and scenes of crime were already busy, and Pinkie could see Warren Mathieson, the head of the crime scene investigators for the Force busy organising his team around the crashed car.

'Warren, I take it this is a bit of a special case to have you out here?' Pinkie asked.

'*Tēnā koe* DS Lumo,' Mathieson said in greeting Pinkie. 'It is very special, come with me you two and see what you think.'

Mathieson walked the pair over to the vehicle, it was a high-end limo. The bodies of the driver and the passenger in the back seat were still in situ awaiting the arrival of the coroner, Dr McCreadie, to pronounce and authorise the removal.

'As you can see the event looks like a simple car crash, but when you look closely at the windshield you can clearly see the bullet hole,' Mathieson pointed to the small round hole at the side of the glass. 'I suspect the shooter expected the glass to shatter, but forgot or was unaware of the bulletproof nature.'

Mathieson walked the pair around to the back rear left window and pointed out a similar small hole. He continued to the rear of the car and pointed to a hole in the side wing near the petrol cap.

'Looks to me like the shooter tried to hit the tank and set the car alight,' Mathieson paused to look at the pair. 'But you two are the detectives.'

Kelly walked back and looked in the passenger door window before calling for Pinkie.

'DS Lumo, have a good look at the passenger,' Kelly stood back and Pinkie looked through the slightly smoked tinted glass. 'Recognise anyone?'

'Oh shit, Jacqui Blackman,' Pinkie exclaimed. 'Pardon me, but we know this lady.'
'Better call the Boss,' Kelly said.

'Yes get a call into him now,' Pinkie ordered, 'and let Charlie know, he was planning to contact her.'

Kelly contacted Barry Goodman and informed him of the victims. Goodman said he was on his way and nothing was to be moved till he arrived, he said he would collect Charlie on the way.

When Kelly returned to the crashed car she could hear Pinkie and Warren Mathieson discussing the bullet holes.

'Do they look like nine millimetres to you?' Pinkie asked the expert.

'Well spotted, DS Lumo, so you were awake at the seminar I gave,' Mathieson took Pinkie to look again inside the vehicle at the driver. 'Judging by the entry wound this was a high-velocity projectile. I would not be surprised if McCreadie finds loads of fragments inside the driver's brain.'

'Frangible bullets?' Pinkie asked.

'Again top marks,' Mathieson continued. 'They may well be, there is a distinct lack of an exit wound and blood. Leads me to believe the bullets or what is left of them is still in there.

I would say from the head wounds, and the fact that the shooter had to hit a moving target, they are very proficient with weapons.

So beware if you approach them.'

Dr McCreadie was next on the scene and set about performing his initial analysis of the bodies and noting the scene. He was a very thorough man and took his time with the work he had to do. Eventually he passed the scene to the CSI photographers to document the bodies photographically.

'Well, Ds Lumo, you seem to be keeping me busy,' McCreadie said as he walked towards the detective. 'I take it Dr Manson is involved in this case I recognise the backseat victim?'
'He's is on the way with Barry Goodman,' Pinkie replied.

'Do me a favour and see he heads home to Scotland soon,' McCreadie said. 'I have noted a rise in the body count since he came to Aotearoa.' The coroner smiled and indicated he was only joking.

Barry Goodman and Charlie Manson arrived on the scene and took a good look at the car and the victims.

'Looks to me like someone was standing on the verge by the passenger door,' Charlie pointed to the area. 'You can see where the footprints were high up on the verge. The shooter most likely took out the driver then moved in to finish the passenger. Who I have to say was on her way to see you three; she appeared in my office after you left.'

'Interesting theory about the shooter, Dr Manson is it?' Mathieson said. 'I have heard quite a bit about you and I have to say I agree.

I am Head of Crime Scenes, Dr Warren Mathieson.'

Charlie shook the scientist's hand and thanked him for his agreement.

'Pinkie, go get Miles Anderson,' Goodman barked. 'Protective custody or arrest him on suspicion, I don't care which, just get his arse in a cell at HQ for now.'

Pinkie acknowledged Goodman's order and left to carry it out with DC Browning in tow.

'Do you think Anderson is involved in this?' Charlie asked.

'Do you?' Goodman replied.

'From Ms Blackman's conversation with me she was scared of someone,' Charlie replied, 'and Anderson is as good a place to start as any.'

Mathieson and McCreadie joined the pair and discussed their findings and thoughts on the weapon.

'Nine millimetres eh,' Goodman said thoughtfully. 'A spooks' choice of calibre, or security service. Charlie let's go bring about that meeting with Standish. I want to see his face when I tell him what he may already know.'

'Sounds like a plan,' Charlie paused. 'Barry, do you have a tech team who could sweep my office for devices?'

'Warren this is your area,' Goodman replied. 'Can you help?'

'Give me the address and I will send the boys over ASAP,' Mathieson replied. 'You look puzzled Dr Manson?'

'Yes nine mill,' Charlie said. 'Could be the calibre that Boss use in South Africa.'
'Whelan is someone else we need to find,' Goodman replied, 'but we need to go after him mob handed.'

-------- 0 --------

Pinkie and Kelly Browning rushed over to the offices of Maxim. They approached the receptionist and asked to be shown through to Miles Anderson's office immediately. The receptionist told them Mr Anderson was not in the office today, with that the detectives asked for his home address and contact details. After some discussion they were supplied this and headed off to the private address they had been given.

Anderson lived in the exclusive side of Sunnynook on the north side of the city and widely recognised as a good area; Anderson's spacious villa was on the good side of that location.
'Can I help you?' the lady who answered the gate intercom asked.

'Yes, it is DS Lumo and DC Browning of New Zealand Police,' Pinkie replied, 'we would like to speak to Mr Miles Anderson as a matter of some urgency.'

'Mr Anderson is not at home today,' the disembodied voice replied.

'Then can we speak to Mrs Anderson?' Pinkie replied, 'this is a murder enquiry and we need to speak to someone from the Anderson family urgently.'

'I am afraid that Mrs Anderson is away for a few days,' the reply came back. 'I will help you as best I can, please come in when the gate opens.'

At that the buzzing sound could be heard which heralded the opening of the gate and the two detectives drove up the long driveway to the house. The driveway was as impressive as the villa that was situated at the end of it. The house was an impressive one storey structure. As they descended from their car the housekeeper greeted them.

'Hello I am Mrs McGowan the Andersons' housekeeper,' the tall elegant lady said her composure holding as she addressed the officers. 'You said this was a murder enquiry, not one of the Andersons surely?'

'No, not one of the Andersons we believe,' Pinkie replied. 'As you can understand until there has been a formal identification we cannot speculate on the victim's identity. Perhaps you can tell us when you last saw Mr Anderson?'

'Mr Anderson left home yesterday evening about eight pm, 'Mrs McGowan replied, he did not say where he was heading.'

'And Mrs Anderson?' Kelly asked.

'Mrs Anderson has been on holiday in Australia for several weeks,' McGowan said with some caution. 'She is not due back for several more.'

After several fruitless questions Pinkie called an end to the interview with the housekeeper. He left his business card for her to make contact should Mr Anderson return.

As they drove away Kelly Browning spoke. 'Did you get the impression she was hiding anything?'
'Not really, too much of a stiff upper lip,' Pinkie replied. 'She does not know where he is, or Mrs Anderson by the sounds of it. Let's get an all ports out for him.'

'I will get a call out now,' Kelly said, then paused before adding, 'Is Anderson a victim or villain?'

'Not a clue, Kelly,' Pinkie replied, 'your guess is as good as mine.' 'Victim,' she replied.

-------- 0 --------

Charlie and Barry Goodman headed back to Police Headquarters. Goodman broke the silence of the journey.

'Jones or Newell can you see their hand in all this?' Goodman asked. 'I mean we are not sure what agency they are with.'

'Not sure,' Charlie was thinking more out loud than answering directly. 'Anything's possible. The next body will be key.'

'You're expecting more bodies?' Barry Goodman sounded shocked.

'Somebody's cleaning house,' Charlie said. 'We have to be very careful; it's the only explanation as to why anyone would execute Blackman. Barry, you need to get people to Queenie's house. She came to see me and shared some insights she may be a target.'

Goodman pulled over and radioed into HQ to get a protection unit to the old lady's home, he also alerted Pinkie to the possibility. Charlie called his sister and asked if Queenie could stay there for a few days. Debbie agreed but speculated that it is Queenie's agreement he needs not her's.

Pinkie and Kelly diverted their journey to Waipu and Queenie's home.

-------- 0 --------

Barry Goodman took out his cell phone and contacted Graham Standish to arrange a meeting ostensibly between Standish and Charlie, but this would allow Standish to be quizzed on the shooting of Ms Blackman along with some other facts about the case.

The group arranged to meet in a park on the north side of Auckland. Cornwall Park is situated off Puriri Drive in the Epson area of the city. It is a widely used park with an extensive history. It was a Maori fortification which was built on the cone of an extinct volcano. There is an obelisk at the centre of the park, near which the donor of the park, Sir John Logan Campbell, is buried. The obelisk is at the summit of One Tree Hill or Maungakiekie to give it its Maori name.

'Barry, thanks for the call', Standish said as he approached the pair, 'and you must be Dr Manson?'

Charlie shook the extended hand of Standish and replied, 'I guess I must be, but I am sure you have seen pictures on whatever file you hold.'

Goodman was surprised by the sharpness in Charlie's tone. This was a side to Charlie, Barry had not witnessed that was more focused and direct.

'Yes, the file does have your picture, Standish replied, and it does speak of a focussed style when in a confrontational situation. I hope this is not going to be a conflict.'

'That very much depends on you, Mr Standish,' Charlie replied. 'I guess you have a full profile on me.'

'We do right down to your recent activities back in Scotland,' Standish replied. 'Oh and that does include the events with Henry Butler in England.'

'So if you have your own profilers, Charlie asked, 'what do you need with me?'

Oh a fresh pair of eyes,' Standish replied, 'some new insights, different perspective.'

'Bullshit,' Charlie snorted back, 'you want an in to Maxim and to know what I have sussed out about Talbot and Newell.'

'What have you sussed out about them?' Standish pushed back.

'Well I have never met Newell,' Charlie said, 'but Talbot has remarkable neat and callous-free hands for a labourer. He is very well educated, and his accent is not quite right. And of course he is remarkably well-developed for someone who has only been around for four years or so.'

'Anything else?'

'Well he comes over as a good second in command,' Charlie stood up and walked a few paces in front of Standish. 'He is a classic enforcer. Shows the strain of having been undercover for a while, but still loyal I guess, and a good suspect for the execution of Ms Blackman.'

'Steady there Dr Manson,' Standish took a step towards Charlie. 'An accusation like that would need to corroboration.'

'Barry, there are a couple of things to note here,' Charlie looked at the detective.

'Yes I got them I think,' Goodman replied. 'Firstly there was no surprise or denial with the news of Ms Blackman's murder. Then there is the encroachment into your personal space a classic Police tactic.

Graham, I thought you did not complete your training years ago. I see that the rumours were true, you were selected for the spook squad.'

'Very good, Barry,' Standish smiled and continued, 'punching above your weight for a country cop. Have you been attending the good Doctor's Summer School as well?'

'No, just well aware of how you lot operate,' Goodman replied as his cell phone beeped that a text had arrived.

'So, Mr Standish, just what agency are you working for?' Charlie asked. 'It's not Interpol as they are not an agency that enforces, so I am guessing some UN political organ.'
'Very good, Dr Manson,' Standish replied. 'To be honest the agency is not important, it is what I can give to the investigation.'

'Like the name of the ship the victims were murdered and dumped from,' Goodman replied.

'Indeed, Barry,' Standish sat down on the bench nearby. 'After all, we are all on the same side at the end of the day. It is a case of cooperation.'

'So you could confirm that our eight bodies came from the 'ULIMAROA' registered in Auckland that travelled from Malaysia to Northport.' Goodman said to Standish's obvious surprise. 'We also have the list of passengers, and know that Newell was a passenger along with Whelan.'

'Very good, Barry,' Standish was obviously taken by surprise. 'Good solid police work.'
'All you can give me now is Newell, Graham,' Goodman replied.

'Ah, not that easy Barry,' Standish sighed. 'That might be a bit tricky. And then there is the fact that Whelan was on the boat too.'

'Yes now that's odd,' Charlie said. 'We have the Chief of Security for Maxim and one of their opponents on a smallish ship when eight people were shot and dumped.

Was it a Navy ship that was on intercept that got the people killed and dumped so that there was no evidence?'

'Old wives tales, Charlie,' Standish replied. 'Never sure what you can believe.'

'Anything happens to that old lady, Standish,' Charlie walked to within a few feet of Standish, 'and I will deal with you personally.'

'Taser me will you?' Standish snapped back.

'Well let's say,' Charlie replied, 'I learnt a lot from Butler. Barry, have we anything else to discuss here?'

'No, there's nothing we can get from him,' Goodman replied. 'We have other fish to fry.'

Chapter 18: Manhunt

The team reconvened with a case conference where Commissioner MacKinnon joined the core team.

'So we know that Newell and Whelan were on the ship that carried the victims found off the coast, Goodman summed up what was known. 'We know that Jacqui Blackman and her driver were killed by a 9mm pistol, as were the dumped bodies. Do we know yet if the bullets match?'

'Not yet, Boss. Forensics are still to conclude their ballistics examination,' Kelly reported. 'They have promised a report within the hour.'

'How's the hunt for out suspects going?' MacKinnon asked.

'Well we have all points out on the four main players,' Pinkie replied, 'Anderson, Whelan, Talbot and Jones.

We have also got a surveillance detail on Standish and a support team covering Queenie's house.'

'The Forensic team found some listening devices in Charlie's office at the University,' Goodman added. 'They are a variety of store-bought devices, nothing we can trace back to a central source.'

'Information on the team watching Standish has to be kept very quiet,' MacKinnon sounded serious. 'If word got out we were watching a Government official we would be in deep shit. What do we know about the Maxim Corporation's involvement in the area?'

'This is where it gets very interesting, Boss,' Goodman said in answer. 'We had the Force's Forensic accounts team do some investigation, their findings make interesting reading.'

'Okay, Barry,' MacKinnon replied. 'Let's have the basic highlights.'

'Well according to the analysts the company based here in Northport is little more than a shell,' Barry said. 'It exists to allow Maxim to own the Northport depot. The owners of the site are actually Maxim Depot Franchise Inc. based out of a Wellington Office that is little more than a post office box. The offices at Maxim in Auckland are actually only rented to the franchise company.

Jacqui Blackman was an employee of the main Maxim group which is a legitimate entity but has no real business presence in New Zealand. Miles Anderson is one of the original directors of Northport Holdings who owned the depot and was taken over by the Maxim franchise organisation. They rent space and provide docking and handling facilities to the Maxim group as well as some other dodgy companies.'

'So, the Maxim presented by Miles Anderson was a bit of an elaborate scam,' Charlie said. 'The profiling of Talbot and Newell were to suss them out.
Jacqui Blackman was about to come clean about the business I suspect, and that is why she was killed.'

'So Charlie, any thoughts on who is pulling the strings?' MacKinnon asked. 'You have met the main players.'

'Trouble is I have only met them briefly,' Charlie replied. 'Not long enough to form any strong opinion. Newell and Whelan being on that boat together is the thing that has me puzzled.'

With that there was a knock on the door of the meeting room and a uniformed sergeant popped his head around the door.

'Boss you wanted to know if there was a hit on the ANRP,' the sergeant said. 'CARMEN has come up with the black Audi registered to Anderson.'

'Pinkie go and get the details and go after that car,' Goodman barked. 'Thanks sergeant if there is any more let us know straight away.'

Pinkie Lumo and Kelly Browning raced to their car and headed off to track the vehicle.

-------- 0 --------

Barry, Charlie and Commissioner MacKinnon walked through to the control room where a large flat panel display showed the area where the hit on Anderson's car had occurred. It showed the main route and also the locations where the ANRP cameras are placed.

Technicians had programmed the display to flash once Anderson's car passed a camera.
The trio watched the progress, and also watched as the police car carrying Lumo and Browning made progress across the city towards the car.

'Where did the car first get a hit?' Charlie asked.

'About a mile from the Maxim building,' a uniformed control room officer replied. 'It appears to be heading into the area known as Sunnynook.'

'That's where Anderson lives,' Charlie thought out loud. 'Do you think he knows we are looking for him?'

'What are you thinking Charlie?' MacKinnon asked.

'He must have seen the news' Charlie said, 'so he will know of Blackman's killing. Why if you have been in hiding do you suddenly break cover and head home?'

'We've police at his home,' Goodman replied, 'he's not stupid he would've worked that out. We're being conned here. Sergeant go and get Pinkie back here, tell him to call off the pursuit.'

'So what's next?' MacKinnon asked. 'Charlie you're the profiler what have we here?'
'Let's lay it out,' Charlie said walking towards a whiteboard on the side wall.

On the whiteboard he put up some headings, victims, locations, organisations and suspects.

Under victims he listed the Peach Cove body, the eight bodies on the coast, the Maxim limo driver and Ms Blackman. Under the locations he listed Northport, Peach Cove and the bay on the east shore of Whangarei.

The list of organisations had Maxim, Eco-Angels and in inverted commas *Security Services*. The list of suspects included Anderson, Whelan, Talbot, Newell, and Standish. Charlie then drew some connecting lines with most having ties to either Northport, Maxim or the security services.

'You think he is heading to Northport,' MacKinnon said. 'It's the most likely place for a suspect to head.'

'I think that's the key,' Charlie said. 'The franchise between the bankrupt company and Maxim is based around Northport. The bodies came from ships that were heading to Northport.

Whoever is behind this is heading there to escape on a ship, I would bet.'

Barry Goodman took over writing on the board. 'All the suspects except Standish have a connection to Northport; whether by an organisation or having been there at some point.'
'If we've just worked this out,' Charlie said, 'why could Standish and the people he works with, who have massive resources, not come to the same conclusion?'

'He said they wanted the local Force to lead on the arrests and prosecutions,' Barry replied. 'Why would they step back from an international crime if they are an international organisation?'

'I can find that out,' MacKinnon said, 'but I think we need to raid Northport.'

The uniformed officers who had staked out Miles Anderson's home arrested the occupants of his company car. These turned out to be two guards from the company's security firm who remained tight-lipped about their involvement.

'Listen you're now suspects in a murder investigation,' Pinkie Lumo was in full flow in the interview room with one of the guards. 'We are not talking one murder, but the murder of nine immigrants, Jacqui Blackman and her driver.

All killed by a nine-millimetre pistol, similar to the one you were carrying when you were arrested. Now ballistics will tell us if they were killed by your weapon. Your pistol may well be a company issued one from a stock which might just happen to be the one, either way you are not licensed to carry the weapon on the streets of Auckland, just at the Northport depot, so actually you are going down for that.

I am sure I can add obstruction and various other offences, so one chance only to help yourself. Talk.'

'I was asked to take the car to Mr Anderson's home,' the guard replied, 'nothing else. As for the murders I know nothing of them and I want my lawyer.'

'Take this gentleman to the cells,' Pinkie said to the uniformed officer watching over from the door.

As the guard left to be placed in a cell, Pinkie sat down.

'What do you think?' Kelly asked.

'You saw him,' Pinkie replied. 'He is well schooled, calm and obviously trained in interview techniques. My guess is military, not sure by the accent whose military he is from. Where do you think he is from?'

'Not from New Zealand that's for sure,' Kelly replied. 'He sounds South African, at best there is a hint of some European dialect there, the problem is he said so little.

But he left so much.' Kelly bent down and from under the table removed the gum the guard had stuck there when they entered the room to start the interview.

'Well spotted Kels,' Pinkie said, 'get that to the forensics for DNA testing and we may get a hit.'

'My thought entirely, Browning replied with a smile on her face, 'and I will get them to dust the table for prints. I cleaned it before we put him in here, so there are just his dabs on that tabletop.'

'Where did you get all this from?' Pinkie asked.

'One of Charlie's Summer School lectures,' she replied, 'I have made it to one or two you know.'

When they met to discuss the outcome of the interviews it appeared that Barry Goodman had not had much success with the guard he was interviewing. He was impressed with the DNA and fingerprint evidence Kelly Browning had spotted. Truth be told, he was a little annoyed he had not thought of the same approach.

Both guards had presented ID but no-one was taking anything for granted, following Standish's involvement in the case.

Charlie had observed Kelly and Pinkie's interview and watched the video of Goodman's but he concurred there was little of value to be taken from them. He did agree the guards were ex-military and not local by any manner of means. Seeing their demeanour, he was sure that they would not be broken by the threat of imprisonment, it would take a radically different approach.

The observation suite had two glass panels on the opposite side that contained one-way glass that allowed for someone to watch interviews discretely. Charlie suggested that both guards from the car be left in the interview rooms. Only one of whom had invoked their rights to a lawyer, which was curious. Charlie sat for thirty minutes watching both men alternatively. MacKinnon watched Charlie the whole time. Barry Goodman and Pinkie Lumo chatted quietly in the corner.

'Can I have a crack at this one,' Charlie pointed to the glass window to his left. 'His ID has him down as Toby Doyle.'

MacKinnon thought for a moment, 'I don't see why not, but why him?'

'Body language,' Charlie replied, 'he is the less comfortable. See how he wraps his arms across his chest from time to time.'

'Yes,' MacKinnon replied.

'He is protecting himself,' Charlie said as MacKinnon looked quizzically at him. 'In an empty room with no threat he feels the need to comfort himself.'

'Your call, Barry,' MacKinnon said.

'We have nothing to lose,' Goodman replied. 'We have got nothing out of either of them so far.'

'How long have they been here?' Charlie asked.

'Coming up for three hours now,' Pinkie replied with a curious look.

'Who's your best conman in uniform here?' Charlie asked.

'Sarge Gallagher, Charlie,' Pinkie replied, 'what are you up to?'

'Take me to him,' Charlie replied. 'I will go in there in a little while but I need the good Sergeant to do something for me first.'

-------- 0 --------

Barry Goodman, Graham MacKinnon and Pinkie Lumo watched as Sergeant Gallagher went in with a cup of coffee and packet of cigarettes.

'Peter Richmond, I have the smokes and coffee the detectives arranged for you,' Gallagher said as he walked to the table.

Doyle said nothing but looked a bit taken aback.

'Oh, this is not Interview Room 2,' Gallagher said. 'Sorry mate, not for you.'

The sergeant left the room and Doyle looked a bit stressed. Charlie entered and sat at the table.

'Mr Doyle, I'm Dr Charlie Manson,' Charlie spoke very briskly. 'I'm assisting the Police in their investigations. I am a forensic criminologist and profiler.'

'I know who you are,' Doyle replied, 'so what is a profiler going to do to me?'

'Doyle sounds Irish,' Charlie ignored the question from the suspect, 'but with your skin tone and clipped accent you're really South African. Which does link you nicely with Dirk Whelan.'

'Any chance of a coffee or a loose, mate?' Doyle asked.

'No chance, they are for those who cooperate mate,' Charlie snapped back. 'And *loose* does also tie you to the townships in South Africa.'

Doyle showed his obvious annoyance. 'Richie is saying nowt, mate.'

'Oh, he's doing a great impression of Miriam Makeba,' Charlie replied. 'No Grammy, but he may well walk out of here yet.'

'Bullshit,' Doyle spat out.

'Tell that to the guards when you get sent to Drakenstein,' Charlie replied keeping up the aggressive tone. I am sure they will find a wife for you there.'

Doyle stood up forcing the table back but the handcuffs and shackles kept him from getting too close to Charlie.

'Sit down man,' Charlie shouted at Doyle. 'You will do nothing, Richmond has already told us you did not tap Blackman, got no bottle.'

'Is that right?' Doyle snapped. 'What does he know; he was not on the boats.' With that he clammed up.

'So you were on the boats,' Charlie pushed the table back slamming it into Doyle who fell back in his chair. 'So you took care of business on the boats. How many did you take out and dump?'

Doyle's eyes blazed at Charlie.

'We know that Newell or whatever he is called took care of business,' Charlie tried a bluff.
'Newell's a pussy,' Doyle replied. 'He chucked his guts over the side when we tapped the trade. Now he's running scared.'

'Well I would run scared from the Triads as well,' Charlie continued to draw Doyle out. 'But you I guess are not scared of them.'
'No way, man,' Doyle sat back and smirked. 'They have to show you their tats before doing anything, all that ritual shit. We just take care of business.'

'We,' Charlie paused, 'ah yes, Whelan and Talbot, you mean. But really you're nothing without Standish behind you.'

'If you're fishing to find out who the main man is, it's a case of very smart, Dr Manson, but no prize.' Doyle clammed up realising he had given much away.

'If I were you I would tell all you know to the nice big detective, who is going to come in and take your statement,' Charlie smiled as he stood up and waved to the glass panel. 'He is your best shot at staying alive my friend, and yes you get your coffee and fags now, if your hands will stay still long enough for you to enjoy them.'

'I want a lawyer,' Doyle snapped.

'I'll bet you do,' Charlie chuckled as he left the room.

-------- 0 --------

'Triads just where did that come from?' Goodman asked Charlie. 'There's been no mention of triads.'

'It's the people smuggling and the sex trade,' Charlie replied. 'Triads are the only thing that fits for the area. If this had been Europe I would have suspected the Russian Mafia or some eastern European group, but down here it was most likely them. So I decided to try a bluff.'

'Okay, I buy that,' MacKinnon said, 'bit of a long shot and you won, but the rest. South African, okay, comes from the accent, but how did you know the pantomime at the start would rattle him?'

'Some of this was long shots, I will admit,' Charlie smiled and sat back in his chair. 'Some of it was down to body language and some down to observation.

Doyle was the more nervous of the two. We could see that from the way he sat in the room, the occasional way he held his arms around himself, suggested a sort of comforting, I put that down to nerves.

His fingers are heavily stained with tobacco, so he is a heavy smoker I guessed that three hours at least without a cigarette and his nerves would be fraying a bit. They both have the stains so that made sure the trick had a chance of working. Your man was excellent. With me so far?'

Barry and Graham both nodded.

'Next, it was time to rattle him,' Charlie continued. 'I figured by taking an aggressive line with him, not answering any questions he put and playing on some South African slang and prison names I could fake him out. Make him lose his cool as they say.
The wifie terms are what they call prisoners who supply others with sexual favours in South African jails, so suggesting that would be his outlet, hit at his manhood a bit.
The rest was just down to playing on the nerves and cravings. And of course the bluffs.'

'Is that the secret of what you do?' MacKinnon asked Charlie.

'Basically, yes,' Charlie leant forward and looked at the Commissioner. 'I guess it is. It's reading body language, observing reactions knowing how people typically react in situations, and how specific types react in those situations, and playing hunches.'

'So it's down to behaviours?' MacKinnon quizzed.

'For me it is,' Charlie stood up and walked to the water dispenser to get a cup of water. 'My particular type of profiling and criminology is based on behavioural sciences.
Some criminologists work on cognitive processes and structure and then others work on linguistics. To me the key is behaviours, it can be learnt behaviours. Under stress and duress we revert to type. The same is the case in high emotional states.
Psychopaths are said to have no empathy or conscience, but what they have are behaviours.'

'Is that what Doyle is, a psychopath?' Goodman joined in.

'No, not really,' Charlie frowned. 'He is just a common or garden criminal type. There is nothing remarkable about him. Works for money. He exhibits fear, which means he is not a psychopath or sociopath. They would not be capable of true, fear yes they can mimic the emotions.'

'So, Mr Big,' Pinkie said from the side of the room, 'have you any Idea who that is?'
'Not yet, but following the logic of who he named and didn't name,' Charlie said, 'the suggestion is Anderson, but I doubt it.'

'So we are looking at Standish or Whelan?' MacKinnon asked.

'Perhaps,' Charlie replied. 'Not sure. Graham there are some unanswered questions. I need to go back to basics.'

'Okay, but we need to raid the Northport depot,' MacKinnon said. 'The key to a lot of this is in that compound, we need to get warrants organised.

Chapter 19: Planning, twists and turns

It became clear to the investigation team that the next course of action was to raid Maxim's depot at Northport. Having seen the footage collected by Colin and Ewan it was clear that this was going to be no easy exercise. The site was heavily guarded by armed by men with automatic weapons. The planning for the raid had to be meticulous and kept secret.

Charlie would not be part of the raid, but would be based back at the divisional HQ building along with MacKinnon. The raid was planned by Goodman, Pinkie and the special police operations team. Firearms would play a big part in the raid. Goodman suspected that there were civilians on that site who could be at risk, so the raid was planned for the early morning.

The briefing session for the raid took place in Force HQ and had a wide array of participants. Staff from the Police, Coastguard, Immigration Service, and local Social Services were joined for the joint operation by naval personnel and representatives from the security services. Charlie sat at the side with Pinkie and Kelly Browning. Commissioner MacKinnon lead the session making quite clear that this was a police operation with support for their partner organisations.

'This is a highly sensitive and complex operation,' MacKinnon sounded authoritative and strong. 'We know that the depot is patrolled and guarded by men with automatic weapons. Two of their number are guests in the cells below and are being held incommunicado.

We have a judge's permission to detain them under anti-terrorism laws, which means they have not spoken to lawyers yet and we can maintain that for the next 48 hours.

The operation will be led by the Police special operations unit who will effect entry to the depot and strike at several of the buildings simultaneously. The Navy and Coastguard are maintaining a blockage on the port at the moment.

Once the special operations boys and girls have secured the building, uniformed officers will support the immigration staff on searches for illegals. Social services will be on hand to deal with any children and sick or ill people we come across.

I am now going to ask Barry Goodman, Senior Investigating Officer on this case, to outline the principal targets for arrest.'

Barry Goodman proceeded to outline the main targets of the raid. These were Whelan, Standish Talbot and Newell.

'We need to find these four,' Goodman added. 'It's highly likely that one of them is our killer. One of them is most likely in charge of the operation.'

'What about Miles Anderson?' a uniformed officer asked.

'He is a person of interest,' Goodman replied, 'but he is not one of the masterminds.

This group are vicious they have killed eight people on a ship, including children, to avoid being caught with illegals. The killings were up close and personal. They have started to clean house by killing Ms Blackman so they will do anything to get clear. So be careful and take no chances. Dr Manson would you like to add anything?'

'Not really, Barry, you have covered the lot,' Charlie looked distracted as he answered. 'Just come back safely guys.'

'Okay guys your section leaders will hand out the operational orders,' Goodman added. 'I want everyone up to speed and ready for the off in two hours.'

Barry watched as Charlie walked away from the briefing and head off out of the building. Goodman caught up with Pinkie and Kelly.

'You two have any clue what's up with Dr Manson?' Goodman asked.

'No Boss, we were about to ask you the same,' Pinkie replied, 'he looked distracted in there. Something is on his mind.'

'Let's go and find out what,' Kelly browning headed off after Charlie. Pinkie followed behind.

-------- 0 --------

The pair of detectives found Charlie sitting on a bench outside Police Headquarters.
'Now I am worried Doc,' Kelly said. 'You look like a man with a problem.'

'It's that obvious Kelly?' Charlie replied. 'Not a problem just some puzzles.'

'Doc what's up?' Pinkie asked.

'It's just that the organisation of the people trafficking seems so well put together,' Charlie said. 'Yet the killing of Blackman and the bodies found on the coast looks like an act of panic almost. Something is not adding up.'

'Any idea what?' Pinkie asked.

'Yes, I have a hunch, 'Charlie replied. 'It's the Blackman killing. I am not sure we have the motive right.'

'I thought we'd that down to shutting her up,' Kelly said. 'Whoever is behind this took the chance to silence her before she could spill the beans.'

'Yes, but remember I spoke to her before she was killed,' Charlie replied. 'She left my office and as heading to Force HQ to speak to someone.

It means that someone knew and they could have been following her and assumed what was going on, but it's a huge assumption.'

'I see what you're saying but we'll never know now,' Kelly said. 'I mean she was down as a victim.'

'Was her home looked over?' Charlie asked. 'Did the team looking at her death search where she lived.'

'Not that I know of, but I can find out,' Pinkie said 'It'll take a while we are going to be busy with Northport.'

'If it was not searched I guess as part of the investigation team you could take a look,' Pinkie suggested. 'I'm sure the DI would go for it.'

'Okay, I might need some help and I know where to get it,' Charlie said.

'DS Lumo,' a voice came from the door of HQ, 'DI Goodman needs you and Dr Manson, something has come up.'

-------- 0 --------

   When DS Lumo returned to the incident room there was a great deal of activity and he could see from the demeanour of Barry Goodman and Graham MacKinnon that something had gone wrong with the plans.

'Boss, what's the problem?' Pinkie said to Goodman.

'The raid is on hold,' Goodman looked flushed, 'we have found Anderson.'

Charlie and Kelly caught up with the group.

'I take it he's dead,' Pinkie said.

'Yes, a bit of a gruesome scene by all accounts,' Goodman added. 'He was found at the back of the Maxim complex in a car park. He had been cut up a bit after being given a heavy beating.

Looks like he has been there a couple of days, forensics are on site processing the scene.'

'Anderson dead,' Charlie said. 'So that takes him out of the frame as Mister Big. This is getting very complex.'

'You don't say,' MacKinnon snapped. 'Sorry to snap, Charlie. This is turning into a bloodbath bodies everywhere.'

'Heavy beating and cut up,' Charlie said, 'now that sounds like Triad punishment.'

'Yes well, to add to that, my sources have come good about Standish,' MacKinnon added. 'Seems he was Hong Kong police till a few years back when he moved to some cross-agency unit. A bit shady by all accounts and there was a theory he had gone rogue.'

'Are the Triad's much in evidence in this area?' Charlie asked.

'Not to any great extent,' Goodman replied. 'They are not very active in New Zealand at all. We are a market they have left alone for the most part. The odd bit of drug activity but the market is too small for them to bother about.'

'Pinkie get over to the crime scene and have a look,' Goodman ordered. 'We will hold off the raid till you have had a look. Charlie please feel free to join him.'

'Thanks Barry,' Charlie replied. 'I would also like to take a look at Blackman's flat.'

'Hunch?' MacKinnon asked.

'Yes something like that,' Charlie replied. 'How do I get access?'

'We have some keys,' Kelly said. 'I'll get them.'

'Can you look on your own Charlie?' Goodman said. 'We are going to be busy.'

'Not a problem, I have enlisted some help,' Charlie replied. 'I'll pick them up on the way.'

'A pair of lycra clad lads, I guess,' MacKinnon said.

-------- 0 --------

When Pinkie, Kelly and Charlie arrived at the crime scene, Dr McCreadie was already on site. The forensic team were busy documenting the scene photographically. Charlie put on the protective footwear and suit he had been handed and walked towards the body.

'Ah Dr Manson, we meet again,' McCreadie said. 'You know that since you have been here I have been busier than I have been for years.'

'I have an alibi for this one, Doc,' Charlie joked. 'I was with these two I think.'

'Were you with them three days ago?' McCreadie asked. 'Because that's most likely when this happened. The body has been here for some time, about the same time as someone was putting nine-millimetre holes into Ms Blackman.'

'Was he killed in situ?' Pinkie asked.

'Looking at the scene and the disturbance I would say so,' McCreadie replied. 'Care to speculate on the scene Charlie?'

Charlie walked around the body careful not to get in the way of the photographers. He stepped in close to look at the body and the wounds. He looked carefully at Anderson's neck where several blows from a machete been made. Charlie paused, then stood up and walked towards the pathologist.

'Yes interesting,' Charlie mused. 'The bruising looks fairly extensive. But there is a surprising lack of blood.'

'Give the man a cigar,' McCreadie replied, 'and the reason for that would be?'

'The chopping injuries were administered post-mortem,' Charlie said, 'not perimortem.

This is not a Triad attack. They do not administer that kind of damage after death. Scenes where they have administered this type of damage would be far bloodier. By the damage to the foliage he was attacked here.'

'Anything else?' McCreadie tested Charlie.

'Yes, looking at the back of his right ear,' Charlie pointed to the spot, 'there is evidence of stippling from a gunshot. I bet he has a bullet in his head and that the chopping injury there was done to cover it up.'

'Do you get much of this type of killing in Scotland then?' the pathologist asked.

'No, but I have done some research a few years back on Triad activity, Charlie said. 'This is something else, another smokescreen I suspect.'

'Yes, there's evidence of an entry wound,' McCreadie said. 'Also there are no defensive wounds on the hands or arms. So either he was unconscious or incapacitated already. Or, looking at the lack of blood, dead already. From what I know, the Triad administer a beating and chops as punishment. They wouldn't deliver this to someone who was dead or so far out of it, they'd wait for him to come round. I served in Hong Kong for a few years.

This is a copycat attack.'

Pinkie Lumo had been looking at the location which was secluded. He walked around and came back to the location of the body.

'No line of sight to the attack,' Lumo looked at the two older men. 'From what I have read they do not hide this kind of activity they would want to make a statement.'

'Good, well spotted,' McCreadie said. 'Now if you'll excuse me I have some work to do. You'll get my report in due course.'

'So someone is making this look like the work of Triads,' Kelly speculated. 'Anyone care to guess why?'

'Throw us off the scent and build a defence,' Charlie answered. 'Whatever's at the back of this, it's not Triads.

The Unsub is cleaning house and putting out false trails.'

'So where does that leave us?' Kelly asked. 'Why make it look like Triad activity?'
'Leaves us looking in the wrong direction,' Pinkie said. 'Right, Doc Charlie, I think I see what you are thinking about the depot.'

'Yeah,' Charlie mused. 'The answer is somewhere else. As for the triads, well, in this part of the world I guess it is the ultimate scare tactic.'

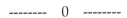
-------- 0 --------

Pinkie and co reported back to DI Goodman and Supt. MacKinnon. The decision was taken to go ahead with the raid on Northport. Pinkie and Kelly would be part of the operation.

Pinkie would lead part of the second wave assault team and Kelly was given the task of interviewing any illegals who were freed from the depot along with the team from Immigration.

Charlie contacted his two former associates from Scotland, Ewan and Colin. They agreed to help him make a search of Blackman's flat. He did point out the supposed Triad activity, just in case the two decided that retirement was far preferable to helping out.

Neither did.

Chapter 20: Raids and Searches

The planning for the raid was finalised and it was agreed that the assault on the depot would take place at 6am the next morning. That gave the teams several hours to go over their plans and make sure they knew what was required. The find of Miles Anderson's body had delayed the raid but on reviewing the circumstances and the initial report from Dr McCreadie, it was decided that the killing was not the work of Triads, but the Unsub's attempt to cover his tracks and scare people off.

The teams took their places. The Special Police Operations team were in position around the perimeter of the depot. Just behind their lines was the Immigration Service. Off the coast and moving into position around the dock area were the Coastguard and a naval assault group. All the teams were awaiting the go from the gold commander Graham MacKinnon.

Charlie sat with Barry Goodman and MacKinnon back at HQ waiting for feedback. He had arranged to meet his two former colleagues at 10am near the residential complex where Ms Blackman had lived, where they would carry out their own search.

MacKinnon gave the go order. The special ops group breached the outer fence and made their way from the east and north borders of the depot to a position some 50 yards from the main buildings. The inflatable dinghies of the naval assault team made their way closer to the dockside and climbed up from the dock to the forecourt of the landing area. Once all the teams reported that they were in position, MacKinnon handed control over to the assault commanders and gave the command to breach the buildings.

The building which Ewan and Colin had reported seeing people within was the first to be breached along with the administration building. The naval assault group quickly arrested and contained the team of guards who protected the site. No shots were fired and the guards within the admin block surrendered very quickly.

The police special ops team challenged the guards who were out and about around the depot. This group did not surrender without offering resistance. A firefight quickly developed, the guards were pegged back to the garage and vehicle holding areas of the depot. The police team took up positions behind some of the large transport vehicles parked in the complex. Once the naval assault team had tie-wrapped the wrists and ankles of the guards within the admin block, some of the naval team took up positions on the second and third floors of the admin block to provide covering fire for the police operations team. The rest of the naval troops made their way out of the admin block to flank behind the garage area and started to fire on the guards' position from the opposite side from the police special operations team.

The firefight raged for several minutes before the special ops commander called for a ceasefire and through a loud hailer addressed the Maxim guards.

'Those within the garage block, I call on you to lay down your arms and leave the building with your hands above your heads,' the special ops commander shouted. 'We have your position surrounded and will treat any shots fired from your position as hostile, and will respond with deadly force.'

The hail from the commander was met with silence. After a very few moments a volley of shots was fired off from the garage.

'Naval support group have you got clear shots on x-rays from your position in the admin block?' the special ops commander asked over the radio system.

'Anyone got a shot?' the naval commander asked.

'Blue one x-ray in the site I have a shot.'

'Blue two no shot.'

'Blue three no shot.'

'Blue four I have an x-ray in site clear shot.'

'Naval commander your call,' the special ops commander replied.

'Blue one and Blue four,' the naval commander replied. 'Light them up.'

Two shots rang out.

'Blue one x-ray down repeat x-ray down.'

'Blue four x-ray down repeat x-ray down.'

'Guards in the garage block put down your weapons and surrender immediately,' the special ops commander shouted through the hailer.

Voices could be heard within the garage block and after a moment's silence the guards within the block opened fire. The noise of the gunshots from the block was fierce.

'Return fire at will, gentlemen,' the special ops commander said over the radio. With that the police and naval groups returned fire. The returned volley of fire was extreme.

Ricochets could be seen bouncing off the garage building around the windows. Within seconds every window within the large structure was smashed having exploded as bullets shattered the panes.

The volley of shots continued for several seconds from both sides, the sound of bodies being hit and screams as bullets found their targets within the building could be heard.

'Cease fire,' the special ops commanded said down the radio. 'You have one minute to surrender or we will continue to assault the building,' the special ops commander hailed the garage block again.

'We will not surrender,' the leader of the guards shouted back, 'but we will send out our wounded for treatment. We have hostages here. Several civilians and will use them as human shields if you open fire.'

The special ops commander looked around to see if there was anyone with knowledge of who these hostages could be. He communicated back with the gold commander.

'He could be bluffing to draw us nearer,' the special ops commander reported. 'What do you want me to do?'

'It could be a trap,' MacKinnon replied. 'We need eyes in that garage block. Can you get any kind of surveillance set-up through webcams or the like?'

The commander asked his technical analyst who said it would be possible, but they would need schematics of the block and about 30 minutes to put this in place. After a few moments he replied to the gold commander.

'We will draw out the removal of the wounded,' he paused. 'That will give us time to get some eyes in the block.'

'Good,' MacKinnon replied, 'but don't take any risks at the first sign of trouble engage the guards.'

The commander ordered the analysts to set about the task.

'Guards in the block,' the commander hailed, 'we will contact you using the phone system to set up the transfer of wounded. Any tricks and we will finish this here and now.

Understood?'

'Understood.'

The commander then set out with his senior officers to plan the removal of wounded and getting eyes into the garage block.

As negotiations went on to set up the exchange of wounded, Gold Commander Graham MacKinnon contacted DS Lumo.

'DS Lumo what is the status of those in the shed identified as housing potential illegal entrants?' MacKinnon asked over the radio.

'Unknown at this time, Sir. We have still to get to the sheds.' Lumo replied. 'I could take a group of officers and try to get to the sheds.'

'What are the risks involved?' MacKinnon asked.
'Going in from the front of the sheds will take us into the line of sight of the guards,' Lumo replied. 'If we flank around the side we could get to the back of the sheds and make an entry through the wooden walls.'

'Okay, talk to the commander on the ground and get a group of officers suited up to go with you,' MacKinnon said. 'First sign of trouble pull back. Do you understand?'

'Understood, Sir,' Lumo replied and went off to set up the action to get to the sheds.

As Lumo's group of officers started their approach around the side of the shed they immediately came under fire from the roof of the garage block. The officers dug into whatever cover was available and returned fire. Two of the police officers took shelter behind the cab of a lorry, as they settled behind the frame of the vehicle an RGP, rocket-propelled grenade, was fired at the cab from the roof, and the ensuing explosion and fire engulfed the officers.

The use of such a weapon immediately brought the cry of pull back from Lumo, and the special ops commander ordered his men to give covering fire. Clearly the guards were in possession of heavier arms than the Police knew about and were prepared to use them to hold on to the illegals in the shed as a bargaining ploy.

'Is everyone clear DS Lumo?' MacKinnon asked over the radio.

'No Sir, we lost two men with the RPG attack,' Lumo said as he raced to safety. 'There was nothing we could do for them, Sir.'

'Okay, regroup with the special ops team,' MacKinnon said. 'We need to plan our strategy.'
'We have eyes in the garage,' the ops commander said. 'We got some webcams in place.
We can see the hostages. They look like civilians, and there is a shitload of weapons.'

The guards had several civilian workers in the garage block who were being held as hostages. This changed the game plan for the police operation.

'It looks like seven hostages in that garage block, and we have no idea how many in the shed,' Goodman said. 'We need to wait them out.'

'Until we can be clear on the weaponry they hold, and the numbers of civilians we have just got to contain them.'

'There is always the option of SAS forces,' MacKinnon said. 'I am loathed to call in the army, but if we have to . . .'

'SAS?' Charlie asked.

'Technically it is NZSAS,' MacKinnon replied. 'New Zealand Special Air Services trained by your UK SAS to their standards, and a damn good regiment.'

'Never knew they existed,' Charlie said with some surprise, 'how about your special police ops?'
'They are highly trained by the SAS,' Goodman replied, 'but not at that level of engagement.

Pinkie Lumo had a twelve-month secondment with the Police Ops Team.'

'You know this does not add up,' Charlie said as MacKinnon and Goodman looked round. 'They know they are not going to get away by shooting their way out. There have been no demands for safe passage, they're just stalling you.'

'What for Charlie?' Goodman asked.

'I am not sure,' Charlie replied, 'it just sounds like they are stalling.'

'Dr Manson,' Sergeant Gallagher said as he entered the control room. 'There are a couple of men in reception for you.'

'That will be Colin and Ewan,' Charlie replied. 'We are going to give Blackman's flat the once over.'

'Take this radio unit with you,' Goodman said handing a radio to Charlie. 'Set it to channel seven and if we need you we will give you a call, if you find anything calls us as well.'
Charlie left to join his former colleagues on the search of Blackman's flat.

-------- 0 --------

As the three men approached the block of executive flats Jacqui Blackman had lived in, they each were stunned by the opulent building.

'Crikey there's money in that block,' Ewan said as they approached.

'Aye there is,' Colin replied, 'but is it clean money?'

'I'm not sure Blackman was crooked,' Charlie replied. 'She certainly was uncomfortable when she came to see me the day she was killed.'

The block was a long three-story building divided into executive flats. Entry was from the ground level garage. Above each garage were two-storey flats of varying sizes. Ms Blackman had a two bedroom flat. Charlie pressed the electronic key and the garage door silently opened to reveal a Mercedes B-Class Sports Tourer, jet black with smoked windows.

As they entered the garage Colin paused. 'Smell that? He asked.

'I do,' Ewan replied as he walked over to the car and placed a hand on the bonnet. 'It's still warm. When was she shot?'

'About 5 days ago,' Charlie replied. 'Who's driving the car?

Do we call for police back-up?'
'Guess we should,' Colin replied. 'But then they are tied up at that siege so maybe we should just go in carefully.'

'You two make as much noise as you can as you climb the stairs,' Ewan said. 'Let's give them a chance to run. I will wait out the back to see if they make a run for it down the back stairs.'

'Sounds like a plan,' Charlie replied.

Charlie and Colin climbed the stairs, talking loudly and making a lot of noise as they approached the door to the flat. Ewan slid around the back of the block to the back stair exit, opened the door and waited.

As they approached the door of the flat Charlie and Colin could hear the sounds of someone rushing around inside and opening a door. Ewan heard the sound of someone making their way down the steps and he started to climb the steps speaking to himself as he went.

'Okay DS Lumo, you lead the way, I will bring up the rear,' Ewan said loudly. He heard the sounds of someone making their way back into the flat.

Charlie and Colin prepared to enter the flat when Charlie's mobile rang.

-------- 0 --------

At the siege back at Northport depot the police commanders were planning their next move along with the Naval and Coastguard officers.

The decision had been taken by the gold commander Graham MacKinnon to wait for the guards to come out. The collection of the wounded had started and was taking some time.

The protocol agreed between the guards and the police was carefully crafted to minimise any contact and opportunity for conflict. The main concern now was for the hostages and their safety.

Kelly Browning and Pinkie Lumo were at the forward surveillance point and were reviewing the video feed from the garage block. They were watching the four monitors that were taking feeds from the webcams that had been placed to give a view of the inside of the garage.

'Okay Pinkie, just what are we looking for?' a clearly frustrated Kelly asked her colleague.

'We have been watching this for an hour now and the hostages aren't doing a thing. I mean even the guards are ignoring them.'

'Exactly, no one has been over to stop them talking,' Pinkie replied. 'Normally they keep hostages quiet. This lot are laughing and talking freely. Charlie was right this doesn't feel right.'

'When was Charlie here?' Kelly said surprise in her voice. 'I thought he was back in HQ.'

'He is but he called me,' Lumo said. 'He has a feeling this is a bit of a show. I know those two officers have been killed but this does not feel like a real siege.'

'And you know what it feels like?' Kelly asked.

'I do,' Pinkie quipped back. 'When I was seconded to special ops, I was involved in a few sieges. This doesn't have the tension the others situations had.'

'Got to admit the body language of those guards looks a bit off,' Kelly replied as she watched the video feed. 'Crap! Did you see that?'

'What?'

'That hostage took something in her hand from the other,' Kelly replied as she looked for a monitor to place back the footage.'

Kelly played back the instance for Pinkie who watched carefully.

'I thought so, they're not even tied up,' Lumo said. 'Get the special op commander.'
DS Lumo spoke with the commander and played back the footage for him and for the commanders back in HQ's gold command.

'Charlie was right,' MacKinnon said. 'Has the man got second sight or what?'

'No, just a bit of knowledge,' Goodman replied. So where does this leave us now?'

'Not needing to call in the heavy mob,' MacKinnon replied. 'The so-called hostages are now to be treated as combatants and the tactics change.'

-------- 0 --------

Charlie grabbed his mobile and quickly answered it when he saw Ewan's name on the screen.

'Charlie, there's someone in there,' Ewan said. 'They were on their way down the back stairs when he heard me and headed back to the flat.

We have them cornered but I think I saw a gun in the guy's hand.'

'Okay stay there we need to think this through,' Charlie replied. 'We have no idea who it is or the layout of the flat.

Do we go in or get back up?'

'Well if we were back on the job I would have said back up,' Colin said, 'but Ewan and I are tourists we don't have to play by the rules. We are not letting whoever it is get away. We have to immobilise that car and keep them in the flat till help gets here' 'There's an apple tree at the back here,' Ewan replied. 'Apple stuck in the exhaust they won't get far if they get out. We need to find stuff to block the doors and stairs.

'Good thinking,' Colin said. 'Charlie get on to Goodman and get back up. If the guy tries to make a run for it, we have to take him down.'

'What the heck are you two on,' Charlie said. 'You tired of retirement or what?'

'Nah, too many bodies to risk this bastard getting away,' Colin said. 'Agreed Ewan?'

'Aye, we go on your word.' The reply came through the mobile phone.

'Okay,' Charlie said, 'I'll radio it into Goodman.'

-------- 0 --------

'Okay so we agree it is a full assault on the garage block,' MacKinnon said. 'We've agreed the hostages are bogus and a ploy to delay us.'

'Okay,' the police special ops commander replied. 'We strike when all the teams are in position, no contact with them till they ignore any calls they try to make. Tear gas and stun grenades through the windows; then we go in.'

'Fine,' MacKinnon replied, 'but hit the sheds with the illegals at the same time, under covering fire.'

'Understood, 'the ops commander replied. 'DS Lumo, you lead that group.'

'Charlie's been on,' Goodman said. 'They have someone cornered in Blackman's flat and are asking for help. I have sent some armed uniformed officers over.'

'Have they any idea who it is?' MacKinnon asked.

'Someone with a gun,' Goodman replied. 'That's about all.'
'Wonderful,' MacKinnon replied.

'An armed response unit is on the way,' Goodman replied. 'Suddenly we're awash with guns.'

'DS Lumo to gold command,' Lumo's voice sounded over the radio. 'Awaiting your go. Be advised that all teams are in position and waiting for the command.'

'The guards have been trying to make contact for the last hour,' Goodman answered the call. 'We have them on edge. I say we go now.'

'DS Lumo, what're your thoughts?' MacKinnon asked.

'Give them a call' Lumo replied, 'to distract them, and then we breach when they answer the call.'

'Good plan. Barry get the negotiator to make the call in five minutes,' MacKinnon replied. 'Lumo, you go when the phone is picked up and be careful.

Take no chances. Deadly force response to any fire coming at you, we are two men down already.'

'Understood, Boss.' Lumo broke off the call and prepared his men.

-------- 0 --------

The armed response unit arrived at the flat, for the last mile or so they stopped their blues and two-tone siren so as not to alert anyone at the flat of their impending arrival. Colin and Charlie met the officers and gave them the run down. Two of the four uniformed officers approached the back of the block where Ewan was waiting.

'Okay Sir, let us take the lead here,' one of the uniformed officers said. 'We'll breach the door when our colleagues on the other side give us the go.'

'Absolutely,' Ewan replied, 'got any more of those flak jackets?'

'Not in your size,' the officer said, 'so stay back till we secure the flat.'

'Armed Police! Lay down your weapons and come to the door,' one of the officers shouted from the front of the building.

No reply came from the flat. The officer stepped forward and pulled the pin on a flash-bang and stuffed it through the letterbox. He stepped back and waited for the blast. The flash and bang was contained within the flat but smashed out the glass panel in the door.

The officers kicked in the door and burst into the flat. At the rear of the flat, the officers there kicked in the door and shouted 'Armed Police' as they breached the flat.

A single shot rang out from within the flat, which prompted a short blast of return fire from the police officers.

-------- 0 --------

'Go, go, go!' shouted DS Lumo.

The assault teams threw flashbangs through the broken windows and forced entry to the garage block once the resounding bangs stopped. Several shots rang out from within the garage block that prompted a reply from the attacking officers. The ensuing firefight was brief, still during which tens of rounds were dispatched by both sides.

'Police. Cease fire,' the special operations commander shouted. 'Combatants within the garage lay down your weapons and get your hands up.'

With that, the remaining guards who could respond dropped their weapons and held their arms in the air.
'Officers secure the prisoners,' the commander shouted.

DS Lumo walked through the garage block, and his eyes were drawn to a group of three bodies lying near the back exit door to the block, blood was pooling from them. He walked over and identified Dirk Whelan, Bruce Talbot and Evan Newell.

The guards who had been holding off the Police and other agencies were tied up; several were wounded, and there was a group of five bodies who had died in the exchanges. Their leader had been separated off and was being led away for questioning. Immigration officers led by Kelly Browning had entered the shed, where some thirty illegal immigrants were cowering behind anything solid to give them shelter from the gunfire. The two guards who had been with them were standing guns at their feet and hands held high above their heads in a surrender pose.

'Christ, take a look at the state of those kids,' Kelly said. 'Get the medics in here right away.'

The scene that greeted them was pitiful. Clearly emaciated and in need of care and attention this was not a group of people who were destined to work the high-end sex trade. These were migrant workers whose future was less than rosy.

Kelly tried to comfort some of the clearly frightened and traumatised children before the medics took over. She walked from the building and headed to the garage block where she was met by Pinkie Lumo.

'So have you got the bastards who were behind this?' Kelly sounded angry, and her eyes were fixed on the door to the block as the so-called hostages were being led from the block in handcuffs.

'Well it was Whelan, Talbot or Newell,' Lumo replied. 'They will be coming out in body bags once the CSIs are finished.'

'You're kidding, all three dead?' Kelly sounded surprised.

'Yes, and not by us I suspect,' Lumo said, pointing at the guards who were sitting on the ground handcuffed and being guarded by armed officers. 'I think this lot cleaned house for someone.'

'Saved us the bother and bullets,' Kelly said. 'Still would have loved to have dispensed some justice for the poor sods in that shed. Pinkie, they are in a bad way.
This was more than sex traders this was people trafficking.'

'I know there is some bad bastard at the back of this,' Lumo put his hand on his colleague's shoulder. 'Kels no-one should have to go through this to have a life.'

'Any word on how Charlie fared at the flat?' Kelly asked.

'Not yet. I am heading to the SVU to give an update to MacKinnon.' Lumo said as he walked towards the vehicle which had been designated as a command centre on site.

-------- 0 --------

Inside the flat, the four armed officers were securing each room and checking for anyone who may be lurking in any of the rooms. No one was found.

Charlie, Colin and Ewan were standing by a body on the settee in the living room area, blood was oozing from an exit wound at the back of the body's neck, and there were clear signs that the deceased had shot themselves through the mouth.

'Know who he is?' Colin asked Charlie.

'Yes,' Charlie replied. 'That is one Graham Standish. He is late of the New Zealand Government, but suspected of having gone rogue and been involved in the people trafficking.'

'Aye well, that's one pension that will not be collected on,' Ewan said. 'Do you think he is the Mister Big behind all this?'

'No, not really,' Charlie replied. 'This is more about organised crime and this guy was just part of the set-up.

I think he took the easy option out. You guys know how the organised crime groups work; he would never have made it to trial.'

'Had you better not contact MacKinnon and Goodman to give them an update?' Colin asked.

'Yes, I will radio this in,' Charlie replied. 'I am sure these guys will have done it anyway, but I will also just now.'

'Okay gents, they tell us you're ex-cops from the UK,' the senior uniformed officer from the armed group said as he walked over to the trio. 'So with that in mind, you will know that we need you out of here and in a secure area while we process you and the paperwork.'

'Actually, we two are pensioners, doesn't that get us out of the paperwork?' Colin joked.

'No chance,' the officer replied. 'You're civvies; just makes for more paper.'

'It's true, police forces are the same the world over,' Ewan replied. 'Lions tied up in paper chains.'

'Christ he's gone all philosophical.......' Colin joked.

Chapter 21: Epilogue

'So Standish left a written confession?' Charlie asked.

'Yes he left chapter and verse on the whole set-up,' Goodman said, 'including a list of the next people up in the chain. Seems at the end he had a pang of the old straight shooter, no pun intended.'

'So what was the scope?' Colin asked.

'Standish met Talbot and Newell back in their days in Hong Kong,' Goodman said. 'Talbot and Newell were corrupted by local crime gangs at the time of the handover to mainland China. They had been up to all sorts for years. Things were getting too hot for them, so they opted for this anti-trafficking group and took their bad ways with them.'

'Where did Whelan and Maxim and their staff come into this?' Charlie asked.

'Well it seems that the local company Anderson was part of was going to the wall,'

MacKinnon took over the tale. 'Maxim was initially a genuine investor, but it was clear that the way they operated, was more of a franchise operation where Anderson got the right to use the name but had to pay a premium for the operation. It looks like he made some inroads in business to start with, but then they dried up, and he looked elsewhere for income. That's where Whelan and the two corrupt ex Hong Kong police came into it. It started out as a sex worker trading operation but slowly became any kind of worker operation.'

'The bodies on the coast what were they about?' Colin asked.

'Well, that looks like the point where Standish got involved with Talbot and Newell.

Seems he had an inroad with groups trafficking slave workers basically. These poor devils paid over what they could raise to Standish, who through Whelan arranged for them to be shipped to Australia via New Zealand using the Maxim ships.

The anti-trafficking initiatives meant that the market for workers was drying up a bit, so the group started just taking the money and killing the people they were trafficking. Once the bodies started washing up on the coast, the game was up.'

'Are they any clearer on who did the killing?' Ewan asked.

'Yes, ballistics shows it was Standish's gun that was the weapon used,' MacKinnon replied. 'His gun as also used on Blackman and her driver.'

'Was she in on it?' Charlie asked.
'No, she was just sent by Maxim to find out what was going on,' Goodman said. 'When she came to see you she was looking to blow the operation wide open. It does look like she was in a relationship of sorts with Standish, and he knew what she was about to do and killed her.'

'So Queenie was right about the slave traders and Bitter Water,' Charlie said. 'You know Commissioner MacKinnon you need to find her a job.'

'She is a remarkable woman, glad she is on our side,' MacKinnon replied.
'The two guys you were holding under anti-terrorism laws,' Charlie asked, 'what's become of them?'

'Yes, well that's a bit delicate,' MacKinnon replied. 'You have your spooks back in the UK. We have ours too.'

'They're not on the side of the good guys?' Charlie asked quizzically.

'No there not good guys,' MacKinnon replied. 'At the moment I suspect they are being held somewhere secure and are being questioned I think is the right term.'

'So best not to ask anymore?' Charlie said.

'Something like that.' MacKinnon replied with a sly wink of his eye. 'Okay gents I suspect that this is shop talk,' Debbie said as she joined the group standing talking. 'I am starting a new rule at the Wakefield BBQs.'

'And what is that, sis?' Charlie asked.

'No uniforms, no cop talk and my brother has to spend at least half the time talking to his family,' Debbie retorted.'

'Point taken. Lads time to scarper!' Colin shouted. 'Charlie you're on your own. Everyman for himself.'

The group dispersed leaving Charlie and his sister alone.

'Now brother you have four weeks left here,' Debbie said, 'how much of that will be with us?'

'As much as I can, Debbie,' Charlie replied. 'I know it's been a bit of a busman's holiday so far, but no more cases.'

'Good, I will hold you to that,' Debbie laughed. 'Mind you, for what it's worth, I doubt you will be able to live up to it.'

'So, Uncle Charlie, what are you going to get into next?' Gisele asked.

'I mean ancient tribal conflicts,' Chrissie said, 'and people trafficking, it has not been dull since you got here.'
'I know, girls,' Charlie replied, 'but I have to do some research and have some time with the lovely ladies of the Wakefield clan before I head back to Cullen and a rest.'
T

hey all shared a laugh and a hug, unaware of the watcher in the wood looking at them through his binoculars.

His focus stayed on the two Wakefield girls...........................

The trilogy will conclude in the near future with **The Prodigal**.

Read more about Dr Charlie Manson
Red Herring
Purified by Fire
Wired
Unsocial Media
Full Circle

Aotearoa Trilogy – Dr Charlie Manson in New Zealand
Family Traditions
Bitter Water
The Prodigal [due in 2019]

By the same Author

From the Dr Richard Kelman Story Book
Past Imperfect [also available as a paperback]

All available for the Amazon Kindle
Visit Dr Manson's Facebook page at
https://www.facebook.com/DrCharlieManson/
Or visit the author's page at : Leslie Tarr's Amazon Author Page

Printed in Great Britain
by Amazon

70280474R00095